THE HEAD HUNTERS

Elmer Carrington, former Captain of the Texas Rangers, is the victim of a horrendous crime committed by the Mexican bandit, Mateo. Accompanied by Daniel Ramos, another victim, he sets off in pursuit of the man they hate. Travelling into Mexico, they encounter terrifying hazards, but nothing prepares them for the torture that awaits them when Carrington is given a hideous task. Failure to carry it out could mean death for them both . . .

MARK BANNERMAN

♦

THE HEAD HUNTERS

Complete and Unabridged

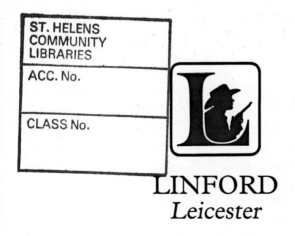

LINFORD
Leicester

First published in Great Britain in 2012 by
Robert Hale Limited
London

First Linford Edition
published 2014
by arrangement with
Robert Hale Limited
London

A catalogue record for this book is available
from the British Library.

ISBN 978–1–4448–2101–7

Published by
F. A. Thorpe (Publishing)
Anstey, Leicestershire

Set by Words & Graphics Ltd.
Anstey, Leicestershire
Printed and bound in Great Britain by
T. J. International Ltd., Padstow, Cornwall

This book is printed on acid-free paper

1

Elmer was in his corral, forking wild hay for his horse. Before he saw the boy, he heard his heaving breath — the sawing and panting of somebody running so fast that they were almost stumbling ahead of themselves. Elmer looked up and for the first time set eyes on the youngster who was rushing down the hill towards the smallholding. Elmer cast aside his rake and stepped outside the corral, closing the gate. He sensed that something unusual was happening.

He was standing by the water pump when the boy came charging in and pulled up, gasping air into his lungs, too tuckered to form words. But his eyes were pleading with Elmer, pleading for help.

Elmer said, 'Steady on, son. Ain't

nothin' to fear here.'

At that moment, his wife Lauren came out from the cabin, wearing her apron and shading her eyes against the Texas sun. She called, 'What is it, Elmer?'

He could not answer because he didn't know. He judged the boy was about fifteen, rail-thin, and Mexican. He had never seen him before. He was bare-footed and his feet were bleeding from the running. His shirt and pants were ragged and dirt-smeared. He had a tangled mop of black hair and his hollow-cheeked face was dusky. At last he found his tongue: 'Help me, sir . . . please.'

Elmer put his arm around the boy's shoulder. 'Come inside,' he said.

The youngster cast a worried glance back. 'They're after me,' he gasped.

Lauren had joined them. 'Who's after you?' she asked.

The boy tried to explain, but his breath caught audibly in his throat. Eventually he said, 'Them!'

'What's your name, son?' Elmer inquired.

The boy looked at him, as if he was deciding whether it was safe to reveal his identity. 'Daniel Ramos,' he finally said.

The three of them went back to the cabin and stepped into the cooler interior. Lauren pressed Daniel onto a chair and fetched him a cup of water, which he gulped down.

'Tell us who you're runnin' from,' Elmer repeated.

The boy's eyes widened. He gazed at the open doorway, as though expecting his pursuers to burst in at any moment, then his lips formed the name as if it pained him: '*Mateo.*'

Elmer felt a sudden chill twist his insides. He muttered, 'Jesus Christ!' and Lauren looked at him disapprovingly for taking the Lord's name in vain. He walked to the doorway and gazed up the hill. All he saw was the green slope and the naked ridge, which were devoid of visible life. The sky was a searing blue and on the high thermals a buzzard was cruising.

Daniel noticed the picture of Elmer hanging on the wall and asked, 'You are a lawman, sir?'

'I was captain in the Texas Rangers,' Elmer said, 'but I'm retired now.'

'You know Mateo?' the boy pressed him.

Elmer frowned. 'Sure I know him. An *hombre malo*. I hunted him for five years. He played cat and mouse with me, and I never caught him. I thought he and his gang had gone south into Mexico.'

'No, sir. They are chasing me. They kidnapped me from home. Last night they were pretty drunk. I wriggled free of my ropes and ran off while they slept, but I know they will have missed me now.' He shuddered. 'They will be after me.'

Since Elmer's retirement, Mateo had haunted his dreams. Now, it seemed, his worst nightmare was being fulfilled. Mateo was a Mexican *bandido*, said to have both Mexican and Mescalero Apache blood in his veins. He and his band had left behind them a trail of havoc — murder, plundered banks and trains, cattle rustling, horse theft, rape and kidnapping. Elmer knew that white children could be traded to the Apaches, either as slaves or for ransom, usually south of the border. The worst thing about Mateo was his incredible delight in torture. It made no difference whether his victims were men, women or children.

Elmer picked up his .44 Henry Repeater. It was said that it was a weapon you could load on a Sunday and fire all week. He slid shells in to the chamber.

'What are you gonna do?' Lauren asked in an agitated voice.

'I'll just take a look around,' he responded and went outside. A few minutes later he was climbing the hill.

Elmer Carrington was fifty years old, his face weather-seamed from years spent in the open, but he was still handsome. His eyes were pale blue. He was a big man, powerfully muscled. Three years ago, he had retired from the Rangers after a career of chasing Comanches, Apaches — and Mateo. He'd hung up his six-shooters and he and Lauren had moved out from Calico Springs to establish their own small-holding here on the Hildago River.

He'd built their cabin with the help of friends from Calico Springs, and hauled a big, black cook-stove from town on his wagon. He had planted out a field of corn, imported a milk-cow, hogs and chickens, and he'd provided a plentiful supply of food with his gun — antelope, wild turkey and venison.

Lauren had chosen furniture for the rooms. She'd made colourful curtains for the windows, and provided her 'woman's touch' in abundance. She was a happy woman, pretty too. Ten years younger than him, she had never been one to nag or find fault, but was a hard worker who was quick to laugh and have fun. They had never had children of their own, although Lauren had miscarried twice.

In other respects, life had been kind to them, flowing peacefully, like the river behind them. However, he had never forgotten Mateo, though he had taken solace from the rumour that he had left the territory and gone south. Now, it seemed, he was back.

Elmer was sweating when he reached the crest of the hill. Before him stretched a huge swathe of grassland, beyond which the rugged line of mountains showed.

Some way out across the plain were ten riders, spread wide, moving in a line at a steady pace, looking like approaching black beetles. Mateo. Elmer swallowed hard, backing down below the skyline. He cursed himself for ever coming to this place to set up home, but he'd got on well with the Indians and offered hospitality to travellers and all had seemed idyllic. Now he was struck by the premonition that everything would change.

He debated what he should do. The intruders should cross the ridge in about twenty minutes. That would give him ample time to get back to the cabin and fort up. Lauren could use a rifle if need be . . . but it would be two guns against ten if it came to a fight. Maybe the boy could do the re-loading.

Elmer knew that if Mateo recognized him, his black soul would be fired with bitterness. Old hatreds would spring up like rekindled fire. Elmer feared not only for himself, but mostly for Lauren.

He broke into a run, descending the hill in giant strides. He passed by the hog pen and the chicken coop and Lauren was waiting for him as he entered the cabin. He glanced around.

'Where's the boy?' he asked.

She shook her head, perplexed. 'He ran out,' she explained. 'He said they would catch him if he stayed here. Last I saw of him, he was runnin' towards the river.'

'Mebbe it's for the best,' Elmer said. 'Mateo's comin' with a bunch of riders.

I seen him out on the plain. We must be ready for him. Lauren . . . load up the old Winchester an' take the window, but for God's sake, keep down. I'll take the doorway.'

She nodded and hastened to comply.

Elmer wondered if Mateo knew that he was approaching the home of his old adversary. If he didn't, it might be possible to bluff him. Failing that it would be a gunfight.

Elmer remembered Mateo as a swarthy, crab-like man, bandy, thick-set and muscular in stature. His droopy moustache covered most of his lower face and his eyes had a predatory quality that was fearful.

Time slipped by in an all-pervasive silence. Looking through the doorway, Elmer's eyes ached with his constant surveillance of the hill's summit.

At last they appeared, and his heartbeat quickened.

They rode over the crest; ten horsemen starting the descent towards the cabin. As they drew closer, he saw that they were all wearing sombreros. He even distinguished Mateo. He again cautioned Lauren to keep well down, out of sight. The intruders reached the flat, and for a moment they were hidden by the barn.

It was then that Mateo's voice called: 'Captain Carrington. We come for the boy. Send him out to us and he will come to no harm.'

Elmer's hopes of being able to bluff the Mexican vanished.

Lauren listened anxiously as her husband cupped his hands to his mouth and shouted his response. 'The boy is not here, Mateo.'

'I think you lie,' came the response. 'We followed his tracks. You must pay the penalty. It will be like the old days, eh? But this time you will die!' and with that a rifle cracked out and the bullet struck the cabin's logs close to the doorjamb.

Elmer ducked back under cover, wondering what form their attack would take.

The answer came quickly — a fusillade of further shots crashing like giant hailstones against the walls of the homestead. After the sudden burst, their ears were singing. In the ensuing lull Elmer risked a quick glance through the doorway. He could see nothing of his adversaries. They had taken cover behind the barn.

His gaze swung to the milk-cow in the corral. Simultaneously, a single shot cracked out and the beast bellowed, crumpled down onto its side and lay unmoving. Elmer cursed but didn't waste his ammunition in retaliation.

After a moment, the beat of hoofs sounded and he saw three horsemen move out from behind the barn, then ride away until they were well out of range of his rifle. They circled to the left and dread grew in him as he realized their intention: to get between the cabin and the river and attack from the rear.

He looked at the pale face of Lauren. 'What can we do, honey?' she gasped.

'When we can see somethin' to fire

at, we'll try to down them,' he replied. 'If we can reduce their numbers, mebbe we'll scare them off.' His voice did not carry much conviction but it was the best he could manage. 'Keep an eye on the front,' he instructed. 'I'll take a look out the back.'

He rushed through the cabin into the back room. It had a window giving a view of the land sloping off to the cottonwoods that lined the river. He grunted with displeasure as he saw that the horsemen had made it to the trees, but a moment later his displeasure turned to horror as he saw the flicker of flame and realized the intent of his enemies. They were going to burn them out!

2

Somewhat earlier, Daniel Ramos had fled from the cabin, terrified that Mateo would recapture him if he remained with the ex-Ranger and his wife. Running madly he passed through the cottonwoods, reached the river and without hesitation plunged in and swam across. On the far bank he glanced back but his view of the cabin was obscured by trees. Taking a deep breath, he ran on, ignoring the pain from his lacerated feet. He had no doubt that Mateo would have followed his tracks and wondered if he would pause at the homestead or would continue in pursuit.

As he ran, thankful of the miles he was putting between himself and his kidnappers, he knew that Calico Springs was some distance ahead of him. He was glad he had learned to race as a youngster.

Ten years ago, Daniel and his Mexican father, mother and two young sisters, had been travelling in a canopied wagon across the prairie when a band of marauding Comanches had appeared as if from nowhere. In a savage attack, the Indians had massacred the entire family apart from five-year-old Daniel. He had been hiding in the wagon when a troop of US cavalry had charged onto the scene and driven the attackers off. The major in charge of the troop was a Texan called John Garfield and he had rescued the boy.

In the subsequent years, John Garfield had left the army and established his own ranch. This had flourished beyond his wildest dreams and he had become a rich man. He had taken Daniel into his family and brought him up with his own children. The boy had grown to his teens in a happy household.

Everything had gone well until one

day when he was out riding on his step-father's range. He had been seized by Mateo and his men. He had been beaten into submission, robbed of his boots and carried off, trussed up like a chicken. If any communication was subsequently made with his step-father regarding a ransom, he did not know. For days he had been dragged along at a rope's end and shown no mercy. But then had come the night when Mateo and his thugs had indulged in their drunken carousal and, while they snored, he had wriggled free of his ropes and got away.

But now, when he glanced over his shoulder, he groaned with dismay; he saw two riders following him and instinct warned him that they were Mexicans. He felt that his energy was flagging. He was pretty sure they had not seen him, nor were they tracking him because the thick, wiry grass over which he had come would reveal nothing of his progress.

Desperately glancing around, he

spotted a gully to his left. Maybe he could hide. He ran to it, seeing that it was bone dry; he slumped behind rocky cover. He waited for what seemed a long time, and then he heard the pounding of hoofs growing closer. He shrank down, not daring to breathe. He imagined that the ground beneath him was trembling with the thud of hoofs. He pressed his hands over his ears, curled himself into a tight ball.

He expected that at any moment the riders would descend into the gully and his freedom would be doomed. But presently he removed his hands from his ears and listened. He heard nothing. Taking a risk, he raised himself to glance around. He was relieved to see that the riders had passed him by. They were no longer in sight, though he could see a distant cloud of dust. They had obviously pushed on towards Calico Springs, perhaps expecting to find him there.

He pondered on what he should do. He still thought it best to get to the town where he might be able to gain help, but he knew he would have to be very careful not to encounter the Mexicans. Perhaps it would be best to stay where he was and wait for nightfall. He stretched out on the ground. He felt exhausted, mentally and physically, and decided to take a doze. Within seconds of closing his eyes, he was asleep.

When he awoke, stars were sprinkled across the velvety blanket of the sky; there was a thin sliver of moon and a coolness chilled the air. He rose to his feet, climbed up the side of the gully and gazed about. He could see no movement in the surrounding terrain, but the lights of Calico Springs glowed in the distance.

Climbing from the gully, he felt stiff and his feet pained him but, gritting his teeth, he set out towards the lights of the town. Now he was obliged to stop frequently for rest. Thirst nagged at him. He remembered the cup of water he'd had at the cabin and wondered what had become of the couple who had befriended him. Perhaps they'd had nothing to fear from Mateo.

As the distance fell behind him, and the glow of lights got closer, he heard sounds coming from the town — the tinkling of pianos and the burble of voices. He knew that his first objective must be the marshal's office. He also hoped he would be able to make clear his predicament and that he could get help. But he had only been to Calico Springs twice before and he had no idea where the law office was located.

He passed outlying cabins from which lamps shone and shortly he reached the main thoroughfare of town — Eagle Street. This had lights illuminating some of the canopied sidewalks and was lined with assorted buildings and stores. There were also two saloons from which raucous sounds and light spilled.

He started along the sidewalk, passing boarded-up windows, anxiously seeking some friendly person who might direct him to the marshal's office. He kept to the shadows as much as possible. At first, everywhere seemed deserted, but then he saw somebody standing in the shadow ahead of him. The man struck a match to light his cigarette — and Daniel glimpsed the outline of a sombrero.

He stemmed back a surge of panic, started to backtrack. Suddenly a voice called out in Spanish: 'There he is!' and boots pounded on the planking.

His heart pounding, Daniel fled down a dark side alley, aware that two men were pursuing him. He had no idea where the second man had come from, but he could hear the jingling of their spurs and the heaving of their breath.

He ran with all the speed his legs could muster, terror giving him renewed strength, ducking along another alley that led off — but then he tripped on a block of wood and went sprawling, grazing his knees and hands. Glancing to the side he saw an overhang in the planking that fronted a cabin and scrambled across to it, seeing a dark hole. He forced himself into it, realizing that he was amid smelly garbage.

With bated breath, he watched as his two pursuers, cursing in Spanish, rushed by and shortly disappeared into the darkness.

He lay still until his heartbeat steadied. He worried in case there were snakes sharing his hiding place. He balanced that possibility with his fear of the Mexicans and decided to remain where he was for the time being.

A dog came along, sniffed at him and moved on.

He waited for what seemed a long time. He had no way of telling the time. He was aware of something nudging his bare foot and guessed it was a rat. With no sign of the Mexicans returning, he reckoned he was ready to make a move. He still harboured a hope of finding the marshal's office, which had to be somewhere in the main street.

Pushing himself out from his hiding place, he took a furtive glance around. All appeared quiet. Moving stealthily, keeping to the darkest places, he retraced his way towards Eagle Street.

When he reached the main thoroughfare, everything appeared quiet — even the saloons — and he guessed the hour was late. He shivered, for the night was cool.

He was about to move off again, when a hand clapped him on the shoulder. Panic tightened his belly in a cold, sick grip. Somebody was standing behind him.

'Where you goin' , skulkin' round this time o' night!' The voice was deep. He turned and saw a big man towering over him. He also saw something else: the glint of a badge pinned to the man's vest.

'You the marshal?' he gasped.

'Sure I am,' came the response. 'Who're you?'

'My name is Daniel Ramos. I was kidnapped by Mateo. I escaped and came here. Mateo's men are chasing me.'

'Mateo.' The marshal sighed deeply. 'Back in these parts, eh? I figured he'd departed long ago. I guess you better come with me, son.'

The marshal, whose name was Tom Henson, led Daniel along the sidewalk and they eventually came to an office from which a light glowed. They went inside. Two men, obviously deputies, were standing by a stove, drinking coffee. Daniel could see that a jail led off the main office but there was nobody in it.

The marshal made Daniel sit down and fetched him a cup of coffee. 'Now tell me your story,' he said.

The other men stopped talking and stood listening. As best as he could, Daniel related his grim experiences. When he explained how the ex-Ranger and his wife had helped him, Henson interrupted.

'That must be Elmer Carrington. Better let McAfee know straight away.'

He turned to one of his deputies, Ben Prebble, and said, 'Go round an' tell McAfee that Elmer may be in trouble.'

'Go an' tell him now?' Prebble exclaimed. 'He'll be asleep.'

'Go right now an' wake him up. He'll wanna make sure Elmer's OK.'

'Yessir!' The deputy rammed on his hat and departed.

'Who's McAfee?' Daniel inquired.

'Captain of the Rangers,' Henson replied. 'An old friend of Elmer Carrington. Took over from him as captain, in fact. He'll wanna check things out. He won't be none pleased about Mateo bein' back in these parts.' He rose and gestured towards the empty cell. 'You better bed down in there, Daniel. Don't worry, we won't lock you in.'

3

Captain Paddy McAfee was as Irish as they come, his voice touched by the Blarney Stone. He was forty years old and slightly overweight. He had been captain of the Rangers for three years and before that he'd been a corporal, serving under Elmer Carrington. He was not very pleased when an insistent hammering on the door of his house roused him from a pleasant dream. He disentangled himself from the arms of his wife and climbed out of bed. He lit a lamp and checked his stem-winder. It was 4 a.m. He stumbled down the stairs to his front door and opened up. Straight away Deputy Prebble imparted the bad news.

At the mention of Carrington, McAfee cursed and said, 'Elmer may be in trouble. I hope to God we're not too late. Tell the marshal I'll rouse my men an' get out there just as soon as I can.'

Prebble nodded and departed.

Within the hour, in the tentative light of dawn, McAfee was leading his troop of six Rangers out of town and heading for the homestead on Hildago River.

As they progressed, the sun rose before them. McAfee turned to his corporal, Bob Justin, and said, 'You smell somethin'?'

'Sure I do — smoke.'

The captain gave a grim nod, alarm gnawing at him. Sure enough, they soon saw how the sky ahead of them was darkened with a spiralling haze of smoke. He urged his men to greater speed. By the time they crossed the river the air was thick with smuts, and after they had passed through the cottonwoods lining the water, they saw all that remained of the homestead — a smouldering ruin.

With heavy hearts, they reined in their horses, feeling the heat that emanated from the blackened timbers. With supports and walls burned through, the roof had caved in. Crackling flames and sparks still plumed upwards and the final wall collapsed as they watched.

Cursing over and over, McAfee spurred around the ruin, his eyes probing for sight of blackened skeletons, but he saw none. He noticed the milk-cow and hogs, all lying dead in their enclosures and coated with flies.

There was nothing he could do here — and a harrowing suspicion was forming in his mind: *his good friends Elmer and Lauren Carrington had been carried off by Mateo.*

The beginnings of tears stung his eyes, caused partly by the acrid smoke but mainly by the grief gripping his soul. By the time he re-joined his men, his grief had changed to a raging hatred for the devils who had perpetrated this evil crime. Fused with a blistering craving for retribution, he ordered the column forward. Seeking tracks in the ground, they spurred their animals up the hill and away from what had so recently been a happy home and haven of hospitality.

★   ★   ★

Elmer became aware of searing pain throbbing through his head. He groaned. Suddenly the vision of Lauren's haunted face came to him — and her screams; they sounded each time she was penetrated. The full horror overwhelmed him and his groan changed to snarling anguish.

'You will watch,' Mateo had told him, 'and you will see her suffer, or mebbe she will enjoy it, and you will remember how you dogged my trail for five years so that I could never rest. When we have had our way with your woman, we will kill her. And afterwards, we will kill you . . . slowly.'

Right then, Elmer had broken free of the man who had held him, hurled himself at Mateo. After that, he remembered nothing. He had not seen the rifle butt descending with brute force upon his skull.

But now, the pain in his head was the lesser evil as memories of the traumatic events flooded back to him.

He could recall how he and Lauren had fled from the burning cabin, having no alternative. There had been no fight. Laughing, the Mexicans had closed in about them, barring further flight with their horses and guns, Mateo foremost. They could have been gunned down there and then, but Mateo had other plans for them. Their hands had been bound with rope, their boots removed, and they had been dragged away, cruelly forced to stagger onwards until the day had darkened and they had come to a canyon. Its sides rose gradually, pitted with deep overhangs and strewn with boulders and rocks, all commanding a view, had there been moonshine, of the canyon floor. It was beneath a particularly deep overhang that Mateo made camp. They were obviously familiar with this place.

Night had deepened, and a fire was

alight, around which the bandits sat drinking whiskey. Elmer was sprawled in the shadowy spot where he'd been felled. As he emitted his cry of torment, Mateo rose and stepped away from his companions and stood over his prisoner, his teeth showing white in a mocking grin.

'It was a shame,' he said, 'the boy got away. It was more of a shame that you did not see all the fun we had with your woman. She put up quite a fight until we held her down. She was mebbe too old to be frisky.' He laughed.

'What have you done with her?' Elmer gasped.

'When she was worn out, I, myself, strangled her. She will not trouble us any more with her screams.'

Black hate consumed Elmer, and with it a rage that shook his body with uncontrollable fierceness; it chattered his teeth and jerked his head. He struggled to rise, to reach for Mateo's throat, but could not; he was bound hand and foot. 'You bastard!' he cried out. 'Bastard, bastard, bastard!'

'Your turn will come soon, *amigo*!' Mateo struck him across the face with the back of his ring-encrusted hand.

Elmer, tied with his hands behind his back, was unable to defend himself. He gritted his teeth against the pain, feeling blood dripping down his cheek. The knowledge that his beloved Lauren was dead choked him. Let them do what they liked with him; he didn't care any longer.

Mateo turned away, checked that the poker he had thrust into the fire was glowing red and grunted with satisfaction. He always carried the poker for opportunities such as this. His motley crew rose to their feet expressing the excitement of anticipation. Having lifted the poker from the embers, Mateo had returned to Elmer, when suddenly there was a disturbance.

A man who had been posted as guard lower down the canyon wall came rushing into the main camp, hissing in

Spanish, 'They are coming. I see them entering the canyon. Rangers!'

Mateo cursed angrily and slung the poker to the ground. In a hushed voice he ordered his men to take up position. Quickly, dirt was thrown onto the fire and the flames stamped out. The bandits grabbed their guns and hurried off to pre-arranged vantage points, disappearing into the darkness. Mateo drew his pistol. He appeared to lose interest in Elmer. He, too, moved stealthily away and was swallowed up by the night.

Now there was a deathly silence. The moon was obscured by cloud and everywhere was cloaked in gloom except for one thing — the still-glowing poker. A wild desperation filled Elmer. Hoping that attention had been diverted elsewhere, a plan formed in his mind. He levered himself across to the poker and turning his back, manoeuvred the linking strands binding his wrists across its hot extremity. He grunted with satisfaction as the

31

smell of burning rope came to his nostrils. It seemed to take an age for the strands to weaken and finally burn through; his wrists were singed, but he ignored the pain and suddenly his hands were free. The redness of the poker was diminishing, but he placed the rope linking his ankles across it and to his relief, after what seemed an eternity, he felt the rope give.

He crouched, working his painfully stiff limbs, his heart pumping. A tiny spark of hope came to him. Had Mateo been lying when he claimed he had killed Lauren? He glanced around and saw the shadowy form beyond the doused fire. He staggered across and found her; his worst fears were confirmed. She was lying with her eyes open, her body already stiffening. He knelt and cradled her in his arms. He'd loved her, always had done, and now she was gone. Angry tears coursed down his cheeks. He should bury her in some secluded place, but there was no time. He gently rested her down, praying that she would understand what he must do.

He rose and all at once heard the clip-clop of approaching hoofs from the canyon below. *Rangers!* He expected at any second to hear the blast of Mexican gunfire.

He realized what he must do. Cupping his hands to his mouth he bawled out with every ounce of strength he could muster: '*Ambush! . . . Ambush!*' And then he staggered out through the overhang opening and up the incline, away from the direction he believed the Mexicans had taken. He cursed, stumbling twice with the stiffness in his legs. He wondered if they would come after him, but he heard no sound of pursuit. He progressed between shadowy boulders and rocks, bruising and grazing himself, expecting at any moment to be shot at. As he went, the roar of gunfire crackled out from behind, but it was not directed at him. He realized that a battle was ensuing. He hoped that his shout had given the Rangers a few seconds to prepare for attack. He also hoped that he would somehow be able to exact vengeance against the evil monster who had murdered his precious wife.

4

Captain Paddy McAfee responded immediately to the shouted warning. It had come from the right-hand side of the canyon and he snapped out an immediate command for his men to dismount and take cover on the left. There was no time to secure the horses and they galloped off further into the canyon. Even as the Rangers scampered to crouch behind the scattered boulders, the crash of gunfire thundered and lead whined amongst them, ricocheting off the rock faces. One man cried out, but he had only been struck in the back by a sliver of rock and soon recovered. The Rangers had all snatched their rifles from their saddle-scabbards as they dismounted and now were quick to take action, aiming their fire at the night-shrouded slope on the other side of the canyon.

The actual place of attack had not been entirely ideal for the Mexicans, as, in response to the shouted warning, the Rangers had taken refuge short of reaching the intended point of ambush; they were thus afforded better cover. Nonetheless the initial exchange of bullets was fierce, the orange spurts from gunbarrels piercing the darkness, the smell of gunsmoke tainting the air.

Presently, the guns quieted. Targets could not be seen and McAfee considered it a waste of ammunition to proceed. The Mexicans must have reached the same conclusion. It seemed that the Rangers were pinned down, because any movement within the canyon would no doubt be spotted by their assailants and McAfee was loath to expose his men. Minutes lengthened into hours as the night dragged away. A cool breeze had the Rangers shivering and, with no water available, thirst plagued them.

McAfee had been in tight fixes before and now he tried to put the present events into perspective. What would Elmer Carrington have done in such circumstances?

The captain pondered on the shouted warning. It had probably saved them from wholesale massacre. It had come from the Mexicans' side of the canyon, and now the conclusion dawned on him. It must have been Elmer. But what retribution had his captors since inflicted upon him?

McAfee tried to form a plan.

It occurred to him that there might be a means of escape behind them. There, the canyon rose more steeply than the other side, but it might be scalable. And whilst it was still dark, such movement might go undetected. He put the idea to his men, and it was agreed that they would attempt it, one at a time.

Corporal Bob Justin was the first to volunteer and he set off with the best-of-luck wishes of his companions. With his rifle strapped across his shoulders, he ascended slowly, taking infinite care to avoid dislodging any rocks. As he disappeared into the darkness, the remaining men waited with bated breath. After some ten minutes, the second man followed Justin.

It took the best part of an hour for the remaining Rangers, apart from McAfee, to complete the climb, but the last man inadvertently sent a pebble rattling down when he had almost reached the top and the captain feared that their movement must have been detected by the Mexicans. Also, the approaching dawn was making the sky lighter which would increase the hazard.

But McAfee was determined to make the climb. He would have to use every scrap of cover. He set out, making good progress to start with. He was halfway up, and could see the cliff top outlined against the pale sky, when a single shot cracked out from the far side of the canyon. He felt a heavy thud in his back just below the shoulder blade and knew he had been badly hit. His fought for his breath, but blood welled up into his throat. He staggered and collapsed. He rolled downward until he was stopped by a large ridge, where he remained wedged.

Above him, his men crouched, alarmed by events. Eventually, with the light growing stronger, they were able to see their captain's sprawled body.

Ranger Josh Simpson suggested that he could go down and attempt to bring McAfee up. Corporal Bob Justin, now in command, reluctantly agreed and ordered the remaining men to train their rifles on the far side of the canyon and to fire at the slightest movement.

Accordingly, Simpson undertook the descent. He was a brave man. He knew that at any moment a bullet might fell him, but he went calmly, sending lizards skittering across the rocks before him. He reached McAfee unscathed.

The captain was lying face down, and Simpson could see the great hole where the bullet had entered his back. Dark blood was caked over his shirt.

'Captain,' he whispered hoarsely, 'can you hear me?' There was no response. He peered closely at the body, then tried to turn it over. McAfee had his mouth sagged open, his wide eyes staring at nothing. A nightmarish certainty struck Simpson: McAfee was dead.

Grunting with exertion, Simpson hoisted his captain's body across his shoulders and commenced the ascent.

* * *

Elmer Carrington had watched the sun rise, painting the eastern ridges with gold. He had paused high on the canyon rim, weary from his desperate flight. His naked feet had been cut and battered by the sharp rocks over which he'd come, but he'd been anxious to put space between himself and the Mexican camp. All along he'd had the daunting sensation of being followed, although he could not be sure. Perhaps, even now, he was being watched. He wondered what Mateo's action had been at finding him gone. Then he thought of Lauren, lying unburied, and he shuddered.

Earlier, he had heard the roar of gunfire from behind him, but that had eventually faded away — after that, nothing.

Suddenly a slight movement, below him and down to his right, caught his eye. At first he was puzzled, but then he realized what it was. A number of horses were grazing on the sparse vegetation of the canyon floor. A surge of interest went through him. He rose, glanced around for sign of his enemies, but saw none.

He hastened along the canyon rim until he was level with the horses, then he began to descend, scrambling from one ridge to the next. Several times he slipped but arrested his falls by grasping outcrops of rock. Halfway down the steep gradient, he stopped to rest. He gazed again at the horses. He counted seven and saw that they were saddled. He recognized them as the mounts of Texas Rangers.

Fifteen minutes later, he reached the canyon floor and, casting caution to the wind, made his way towards the animals. They raised their heads at his approach, whickering nervously. He paused, standing still as they grew used to his presence and resumed grazing. Then he walked up to the nearest, murmured calming words and reached out to gently smooth its withers. He grasped the reins, was about to haul himself into the saddle when the shot came.

He felt a sharp slam of pain just below his knee and his leg gave out. As he collapsed, he was aware that the horses had stampeded off, scared by the crack of the gun. His pain seemed to increase in throbbing waves. And then he heard oncoming footsteps and the gurgle of laughter.

'Mateo said, 'Bring him back alive',' a Mexican voice pronounced, 'So I just shoot you in the leg so you can't run away again. You are lucky, eh? For the moment. Maybe I shoot you in the other leg too! That would be good, *amigo*.'

Elmer raised his eyes, realized the man was standing over him — a scrawny greaser with a leer on his face. His pistol was levelled unwaveringly. He appeared to be alone. He must have been coming up the canyon floor and had spotted Elmer as he approached the horses. Elmer grimaced with pain, conscious that blood was pumping out from his wound.

'Get up, or I plug the other leg!' the Mexican said.

Elmer cursed his luck. If only he'd stayed on the canyon's rim. He pushed himself into a sitting position, and attempted to rise. He couldn't make it and collapsed. That was when another shot boomed off, coming from behind him.

The Mexican was thrown back; the bullet had struck him in the chest bringing forth a great spurt of blood. He lay on his back, a single shudder going through him. His breath came in a hoarse rasp, then it weakened and stopped altogether.

He was dead.

Elmer glanced over his shoulder and gasped with relief. Two Rangers, Corporal Bob Justin and Ranger Clay Forrester, were hurrying towards him, their rifles held in readiness. They had both been serving when Elmer commanded the troop and he knew them well. They had come to round up their horses; their arrival had certainly been opportune. Seconds later they were with him, expressing surprise at finding him.

Elmer uttered his profound gratitude at being rescued.

While Forrester kept watch, Justin unfastened his bandanna and tied it tightly around Elmer's leg to form a tourniquet above the knee. 'You need a doctor, Captain, as soon as we can get you back to town. Let's hope he can save your leg.'

'Where's Mateo?' Elmer asked.

'I guess them bandits pulled out during the night,' Justin explained. 'We had a shoot-out with them, but after a while things went quiet. We took a scout-see this mornin' , found their camp and they'd all gone.'

'Gone?' Elmer queried.

'Sure,' Justin nodded. 'Pulled out while it was still dark, I guess. We also found the cave where they'd left their hosses.'

Elmer's next words came with obvious grief. 'When you went to where they'd camped, did you find . . . did you find my wife's body?'

Justin frowned. 'Why no. We didn't know she was . . . dead.' He reached out and gave Elmer's shoulder a sympathetic pat. 'I'm downright sorry, Captain.'

Elmer said, 'Mateo raped her then strangled her.'

For a moment the two Rangers were wordless with disgust.

While they were helping Elmer across to the shelter of boulders at the foot of the far canyon wall, they told him that Captain McAfee had also died and Elmer shook his head in dismay and experienced renewed sorrow. His wife and now his friend — dead.

Mateo had much to answer for.

They left Elmer seated in shadowy cover with a gun in his hand, then went to round up the horses. Gritting his teeth against his pain, Elmer kept a wary eye open, but he saw no movement apart from the turkey vultures that had descended to rip out the entrails of the Mexican; in time they and other scavengers would reduce the corpse to a skeleton.

Somewhere in the background a woodpecker was hammering on an elm.

He guessed that when Mateo had pulled out, he had left the one man to hunt him down, but that man had been thwarted, thank God.

When the two Rangers returned, driving the herd before them, they assisted Elmer into the saddle; this was difficult at first because he couldn't put the foot of his injured leg into the stirrup. Forrester recovered the pistol from the dead Mexican so Forrester could determine the calibre of bullet that had hit Elmer. Now, with all three men astride their mounts, and herding the recovered animals, they set off to rejoin the other Rangers.

It took three hours for the dejected troop, bearing the body of their captain, to reach Calico Springs. They'd travelled with the depressing knowledge that Mateo had eluded them and was still at large to vent havoc wherever he chose, and the cost had been high. For Elmer, every jog over the ground brought fresh waves of torture to his wounded limb, causing pain to seep up through his thigh into every cranny of his body, and his head still throbbed from the blow it had received. Added to which he felt a fever taking hold of him. Even so, right then, the greatest pain he suffered was in his heart.

5

Doctor Silas Hathaway was a portly man of sixty-five, wearing wire-rimmed spectacles. His hair had already turned white and his rosy-cheeked face showed an excess of flesh. He had served as a surgeon-physician in the Confederate States Army and was no stranger to amputations.

Yesterday when Elmer had first been brought to his small infirmary at Calico Springs, he'd removed the blood-soaked tourniquet and dosed his patient with laudanum. He'd then washed out the wound and the sucked-in clothing. Afterwards, he'd applied a bandage, having noted the .35 calibre bullet had buried itself in the leg, fracturing the tibia, tearing muscle and tissue and leaving a large entry hole.

Today he'd removed the bandage and examined the limb again. He frowned.

Elmer, clad in a nightshirt, was resting back on the surgery couch. He didn't miss Hathaway's grim expression.

'I won't lose the leg, will I?'

'It would only be from below the knee,' the doctor said, half to himself.

Elmer felt woozy with fever and laudanum.

The medical man leaned close to the wound. He sniffed, wrinkling his nose. 'Sure doesn't smell so good, Captain.'

Elmer, too, had noticed the sweetish, fetid odour and his stomach churned. He risked a downward look, catching a glimpse of greenish flesh.

'Putrid,' Hathaway announced.

Elmer groaned. 'It ain't gonna kill me, is it, Doc?'

'Not if you receive the right medical treatment straight away.'

★　★　★

Once Mateo had lost the element of surprise, he had tired of the engagement with the Rangers and had slipped away into the night. Before he had quit the canyon campsite, he had had a hole dug; the body of the woman was dropped into it and covered over. He had left the grave as indistinguishable as possible. If anybody chose to search for it, they would have a difficult task.

He was still furious at losing both the boy and Carrington. He had vented his rage by bullying his six men. The reason they stuck with him was greed, for he offered the prospect of ill-gotten fortune. Gradually, Mateo lost hope that the *hombre* he had despatched to recapture the *gringo* captain would bring him back.

But now he set his mind on new business, business involving *mucho dinero.*

He enforced a stiff pace as the gang rode south, crossing tortile mountains and arid desert where the heat was nigh suffocating. They were a ragged, unshaven bunch, disinclined to wash even when water was available, and dangerous as rattlesnakes. Heavy pistols sagged in holsters from their waists, also long knives. The only sign of civilization they encountered came from defunct ghost towns, relics of long-gone mining communities, in which the sole movement was the wind-blown tumbleweed, rolling down forsaken streets.

Three weeks later found them camped in a canyon in the foothills of the Sabine Mountains, close to where the Smith & Atchison Railroad went into a sharp curve. The Red Rock Express passed along this track every night. Mateo had long cherished a dream of hitting the train when it was loaded with miners' pay, reputedly at the end of each month.

The bandits made their plans as they waited for the appointed time to arrive. Mateo kept a sweat-soiled calendar on which he ticked off the passing days. On the evening of August 31, they stacked cross-ties high on the track where the curve was at its most acute and took cover in adjacent boulders.

They were not disappointed.

The Red Rock Express arrived at 11 p.m., right on schedule. Firstly, they heard the hum and clack of wheels on the narrow-gauge roadbed, then the plaintive call of its whistle. Suddenly, as the train rounded the bend, the swinging beam of the locomotive's lamp, backed by the bloody glow from the firebox, cleaved the darkness. The panicking engineer, glimpsing the piled-up obstruction, slammed on his brakes and brought the train to a shuddering halt with its cow-catcher touching the wood.

Hoisting their bandannas into place, the Mexicans sprang into action, two men splitting off to discourage any vigilante passengers from trying to be heroes while at the same time relieving them of their valuables, and another departing to attend to the engineer and fireman. Meanwhile Mateo and his remaining two bandits pulled themselves up onto the vestibule of the express car. Mateo hammered on the slide door with his fist and yelled out, 'We dynamite you if you don't open up!'

Almost immediately the door was drawn back and a man barred the way, an angry-looking man in a blue cap and with a carbine in his hands. Before he could aim it, Mateo's pistol blasted off, killing the railroad man and clearing the way. All the bandits entered the car, where two company employees were staggering to their feet, their eyes wide with fear. They straight away dropped their guns and raised their hands, having no stomach for a fight.

'Open up the safe or you die!' Mateo snarled.

'Sure — don't shoot.'

Within seconds the safe was manipulated and its door swung open to reveal dollar bills, stack upon stack of them. Their hands trembling with excitement, the Mexicans scooped the money into the sacks they'd brought. As they prepared to leave, Mateo turned his hawk-eyes towards the two cowering railroad men. Fearing what was to come, they started pleading for their lives, but Mateo raised his gun and shot them both, killing them instantly. As he and his men were backing out, a shot sounded from the foremost passenger car.

Two bandits had gone to attend to the passengers; only one, a sack of valuables over his shoulder, reappeared. As he ran off into the darkness, another shot followed him but missed. A man in army uniform stood at the train's open window, brandishing his pistol. He'd already shot one bandit who was sprawled bleeding in the aisle behind him.

Mateo and his gang didn't waste further bullets, but sped off, carrying their spoils. They reached their horses, mounted, and then concentrated on putting as much distance as they could between themselves and the plundered train. As well as the two men that Mateo had killed, the engineer had also been gunned down. In the aftermath of the robbery, the railroad company confirmed that $100,000 had been stolen from its safe, and some $2,000 taken from the passengers — wealthy ranchers who had attended a stock-men's convention in Culver City. Four employees had been murdered.

The State Governor ordered out militia and cavalry. They curry-combed the territory, but to no avail. The birds had flown.

6

The boy Daniel Ramos had returned to his home by stagecoach, escorted by one of the Calico Springs deputies. His grateful step-parents and step-brothers and sisters welcomed him with open arms. During the following months, John Garfield would never let Ramos ride the range alone; he was always accompanied by himself or one of the ranch-hands. While Daniel had been missing, Garfield and his ranch-hands had combed the range and eventually concluded that the boy had been abducted. The matter had been reported to the law but no information regarding those guilty had been forthcoming. With the boy's return, a great deal was revealed. Garfield referred the matter once again to the local marshal; 'Wanted' notices for Mateo and his gang were circulated far and wide and a cash reward put up by the rail company, dead or alive.

As if to flaunt those who hunted them, news came through, by telegraph and newspaper reports, regarding the gang's hold-up of the Red Rock Express and the killings that had taken place. Although the robbers' faces had been concealed, the passengers had no doubt as to the identity of their Mexican persecutors.

With the onset of winter, and a chilly wind blowing from the north, Daniel accompanied his step-father on a tour of the line camps, dotted on the farthest ranch boundaries. These consisted of crude shacks where cowboys stayed alone. Their duties were to patrol the range in their area, to herd outfit cattle back, to chase strays away, to discourage rustling and to repair fences. Alone for so many hours, the cowboys were always anxious for a chinwag over a mug of coffee and Daniel loved to hear their stories and the exchange of humour with his step-father.

John Garfield was normally a hale

and hearty man, liked by all. But today Daniel noticed that he was quieter than usual. Of late, he had complained of not feeling well but had put it down to indigestion.

* * *

As they set out on the return journey he was sweating despite the cold wind and suffering from shortness of breath. When they were almost home, he suffered agonizing pain down his left side, radiating into his arm. He slumped forward in his saddle, his face contorted. He collapsed heavily onto the ground. Daniel reined in and dismounted, running to his step-father's side.

Garfield lived for only a few minutes more, long enough to reach out and clutch Daniel's hand. He tried to speak but a jolt of agony cut his breath, choking him.

'Don't die, Papa,' Daniel pleaded, but it was in vain. Tears were streaming down the boy's cheeks as John Garfield left for the next world.

Daniel's step-mother, Amelia, inherited the prospering ranch and its extensive stock. She grieved for her husband. Soon she found the duty of running the outfit too heavy for her. The new foreman, Buck Wallace, whom John had taken on shortly before his death, was paying her increasing attention. Indeed, he was soon taking over most of the chores.

Wallace sometimes seemed a rough customer, a burly, florid-faced man who liked his whiskey. But he knew the cattle business and towards Amelia he showed a kindness and gentleness to which she responded, prettifying herself and paying renewed attention to her hair and dress. Shortly he had moved in to the main house. Within a month they were married and she became pregnant.

As for Daniel and the other youngsters, Wallace showed them none of the kindness he reserved for Amelia. In fact, he clearly resented Daniel and allotted him the most menial tasks to do on the ranch. Furthermore, the boy grew fiercely jealous as his step-mother focused all her considerations on her husband.

By the time spring came round, Daniel's mood had plunged to deep melancholy and he became determined to run away.

★　★　★

Elmer had changed from the cool, prudent man he had once been. His wife and his friend had been murdered, and despite the cunning he had learned as a Texas Ranger, there now rose in him the impetuous and hateful rage of a man who had been deeply wronged. No people, no lawmen, could ever assume his responsibility of retribution. With his home destroyed he had no meaningful place to go now, but this did not bring an emptiness to his life. Any void was filled by the cold conviction that Mateo must die, and that he, Elmer

Carrington, must do the killing.

In the first instance, after Doctor Hathaway had carried out his surgery, when laudanum still had him drifting in a dream-world, he found that he had his hands around Mateo's throat and the squeezing of his windpipe created a choking, and a bulging of the Mexican's eyes so that they looked like two onions. His tongue, purple in hue and coated with scum, hung loosely from his gaping mouth.

Elmer dragged himself from the dream and came round in a flurry of sweat.

In more rational moments, he tried to make plans as to how he could achieve such a situation. The immediate need was to regain some fitness. He was under no illusions as to the seriousness of his injury.

Doctor Hathaway had shown him a small and mangled piece of lead around which a fragment of cloth was still wrapped. 'You're a dead lucky man,' Hathaway had said. 'The bullet was deeply embedded. I probed into the wound, dug a great hole and got it out. It'd taken a scrap of your pants with it and it had all gone mouldy, but I swabbed away the poison.' He allowed himself a satisfied smile. 'I guess a less capable surgeon would never have reached it. It'd compromised your entire blood circulation, caused the infection.'

Elmer eyed his leg and grimaced, but he said, 'I'm right grateful to you, Doc. No words are enough to say how grateful.'

'I'm not promising you'll keep that leg,' the doctor cautioned. 'We'll let it drain for a few days, then I'll get a splint on it. It may still turn bad, but let's pray for the best.'

'I'll sure do that, Doc.'

And pray Elmer did, so emphatically that over subsequent weeks the wound healed and the splint straightened the leg, but he could not put his foot to the ground because it caused him considerable pain. Hathaway warned him he would never be pain free. 'But I'll be downright annoyed if you go and get yourself killed,' he added. 'I've not done all that surgery for nothing!'

★　★　★

Despite the wearisome, blistering travel, the bandits were gratified by thoughts that wealth was now theirs. By the time they made camp in a remote Maroma Mountain hollow, they had replenished their supply of liquor from a wayside cantina, and were in high spirits, particularly Mateo. They had fed on the juicy flesh of the goat they had killed and now they were downing snakehead whiskey to excess. They sat around, their greedy eyes glinting in the firelight, as Mateo took on the task of splitting the plundered cash. In the past, it had been his custom to keep the major share of any loot for himself, leaving them the minimum amount that would stave off their dissatisfaction. He'd relied on their fear of his explosive temper to quell complaint. But tonight everything seemed different as he smilingly doled out a more than fair allocation to each of his six remaining followers.

When the task was completed, the cash was stowed away in saddle-bags and the mood got riotous as more rot-gut was consumed. There was talk about the gang scattering and meeting in Mexico in a year's time, but any decision would have to wait till morning. One man produced a mouth organ he had lifted from a train passenger and this signalled a raucous sing-song, but after a while tiredness overtook them. A pine knot was placed on the fire, and three of them retired to their blankets, not giving a fig about the threat of waking with thick heads.

But Mateo was not tired. Excitement pulsed through his veins hotter than liquor. While giving the impression of drinking heavily like the others, he had downed only enough to satisfy his immediate lust. He surreptitiously removed his spare pistol from his saddle-bag and slipped it into his waistband, then he rose and stepped away from the campsite.

Once in the trees he took out both the spare Colt .44 and the one holstered at his hip. He checked that each was fully loaded. They were big six-shooters that could fire rapidly. He smiled his wolfish grin, feeling renewed exhilaration as he paced back to the campsite.

He opened up with a fusillade of lead. He fired from both hands, thumbing back the hammers, the guns booming like cannons. The only man still seated at the fireside took a bullet in the back, spurting blood as he was thrown headfirst into the flames. The remaining blanket-huddled Mexicans struggled up, but the heavy-calibre bullets tore into them, gunning them down before they could reach for their own weapons. The air was filled with the thunderous roar of the guns and the frantic screams of men, and everywhere was hazed in the swirl of acrid smoke.

At last Mateo paused, breathing heavily from his efforts — but his work was not finished.

He inspected each body, checking for life. He saw faint movement in one man and groans came from another. He pressed a pistol to their heads and blew out their brains.

Afterwards, he holstered his guns. Kicking aside the corpses, piled one upon the other, he extracted from their saddle-bags the cash that he had so recently distributed. This he carefully packed into his own saddle-bags, buckling them tightly.

He retrieved his sombrero, took a final swig from a whiskey jug, then, his tack on his shoulder, he went to the spot where the horses were hobbled. They were still agitated by the recent gunfire but he soothed them with calming words. He cut the rawhide hobbles with a slash of his knife. He could not tolerate animals being left to suffer. It was better to let them roam free. He saddled his own big roan, mounted and rode out into the night, bound for Mexico, where US law had no jurisdiction. He was a wealthy man.

But he had overlooked one fact. When he had stepped away from the campsite, one of the gang, Luiz Prado, had also gone into the brush — to relieve himself. He had watched the killings, including that of his brother, with petrified eyes and then he had run off, thanking the Holy Saints that he had survived Mateo's treachery.

7

When Elmer was strong enough, he left Doctor Hathaway's small infirmary and took up lodgings at The Golden Sunrise Guesthouse on Main Street, Calico Springs. If he put his foot down, he suffered pain, could not move around far without the aid of a crutch. However, he worked hard on the exercises that the doctor recommended and he knew he was growing stronger each day. He needed to form a plan for his future. At least he had no financial worries. He had inherited a tidy sum of money from his father and this was safely deposited in the town's bank. But he found little satisfaction in this, for he was still burdened with sorrow, would always be, at the loss of Lauren.

Weeks after taking up residence at the guesthouse, he was visited by Bob Justin. He was jubilant. Notification had come through from the Texas Rangers Headquarters at Austin that he had been promoted to captain to replace Paddy McAfee. Elmer congratulated him, knowing the elevation was justly deserved.

As they were drinking coffee, the Ranger produced the lurid report of the train robbery in an old copy of *The Texas Chronicle*. Hatred burned deep in Elmer's heart as he read Mateo's name. The crime had been committed beyond the borders of Texas, and was not, therefore, within the Rangers' area of responsibility, but it cemented Elmer's resolve to kill his wife's murderer.

The thought that Lauren had died in the most hideous of circumstances and her remains dumped somewhere unknown had haunted Elmer's nightmares. The last point of contact had been in the canyon hideaway where Lauren had perished, and Justin agreed to help him find it.

Next morning they hired a springboard wagon and mare from the local hostelry and set out on their quest. It was a tedious and bumpy ride through rock-strewn canyons, some of which were choked with autumnal brush leaving a passageway too narrow to drive the wagon through; they were thus caused to divert. Despite the lateness of the season, the air was swarming with flies.

After hours of travel, both men recognized familiar rock shapes and canyon walls and knew they had arrived at the site of the gun battle. Elmer felt a shiver pass through him as he recalled the appalling events that had occurred here. Even now, he glanced at the high rims with apprehension, fearing that he might be within the sights of a hidden marksman. Could Mateo, knowing that he would return to this place, be waiting for him? He shrugged the thought away.

There was over everything a brooding silence. Not even a buzzard cruised on the high thermals. They halted the wagon at the side of the canyon and proceeded on foot, leaving the mare cropping at the thin grass. Elmer struggled bravely, using his crutch, crawling some of the way. Soon they were scrambling up the steep incline, clinging to outcroppings of rock for support. They reached a grassy plateau, backed by a gaping cave and Elmer knew immediately that this was where he'd been held captive and where Lauren had been murdered.

It was quite possible that his wife's body had been disposed of elsewhere, but he knew he would not rest until this place had been searched.

The two men separated, and for hours moved far and wide, seeking any sign of a burying, Elmer hobbling manfully. They even searched the gloomy depths of the cave.

Daylight was starting to fade and they were about to admit failure, when Elmer spotted a patch of earth that had been deeply scratched. At first he was puzzled but then concluded that this was where a coyote or other creature had attempted to dig, attracted by some scent. His heartbeat quickened. He called to Justin who joined him and agreed that this could be a grave.

The Ranger descended to the wagon and returned with a spade and a blanket. He began to dig, Elmer being too handicapped to assist, and presently the remains of a human hand were unearthed. The air thickened with the sickly stench of decay. Elmer waved away the swarm of flies that suddenly pestered them, and nausea enveloped him. They had found what he sought, yet the finding left him wanting to die.

He steeled himself, gritted his teeth and wiped away the tears that were blurring his eyes. Both men raised bandannas over their noses as Justin dug on. Soon the corpse was uncovered, seething with maggots and worms. It might have been unrecognizable had it not been for the familiar pattern of the rotting dress.

They raised what was left of his beloved Lauren from her makeshift grave and wrapped her in the blanket. Cradling her in his arms, finding her feather-light, Justin led the way down the treacherous slope, fanning away flies as he went. They gently rested her on the bed of the wagon and re-loaded the spade. Ten minutes later, with dusk deepening, they started back for Calico Springs. They arrived in the early hours of the following morning.

Elmer had Lauren attended to by an undertaker. He had a fine coffin made, and she was re-interred in the town's cemetery. Watched by a circle of friends, the local minister spoke words of tenderness and love and a hymn was sung. Elmer had a headstone erected with a simple inscription. He felt that a chapter had been closed.

But he swore it was not the *final* chapter.

★   ★   ★

The boy Daniel Ramos had come upon the farm late in the day. He was ravenous, not having eaten for forty-eight hours. He was also dog-tired. He had run away from home two weeks earlier, having left a note for his step-mother: *Gone to join Texas Rangers. Will make my own way from now on.*

He'd had no money as he set out on foot, camping rough or sometimes finding shelter in a barn or deserted shack. It was springtime, but summer warmth showed no sign of appearing and at night he shivered. He lived mostly off any scraps he could beg or steal from farms or smallholdings. Once, with an improvised catapult, he killed a squirrel and ate it raw. He had also tried to catch a snake but it eluded him. He drank from streams. He trudged southward across hills, sometimes finding sustenance and company in travelling pedlars who took mercy on the rail-thin youngster.

There were occasions when he regretted leaving his home, for there he had had a bed to sleep in and food to eat, but then he would recall that his step-father was no longer there, his place having been taken by a man he could not abide — and he realized he would never go back.

And now he had come upon this large farm where there were a cultivated meadow, penned hogs and chickens and two horses in a corral. Utterly weary, his belly rumbling with hunger, he crept around a shadowy barn. Off to his left was a broken plough. Nobody seemed to be about. Dusk was deepening. He crossed the yard, approached the house. A door was standing open and he glimpsed the kitchen within.

He crept forward, desperation suppressing his fear. Through the doorway he could see a table on which a lamp glowed. There were also a half-eaten chicken, a loaf of bread and a large milk-jug. Nobody was in the kitchen, but he heard voices coming from another part of the house. Glancing around, he satisfied himself that he was unobserved, then he made his entry.

The proximity of the food crumbled his last hesitation. He lifted the jug and took a long swig of creamy milk. At that moment footsteps sounded, approaching from within the house. He grabbed the chicken and bread. He darted outside and spotted a man tinkering with the broken plough, his back turned. Daniel fled like a shadow across the yard to the only place of concealment he could see — the barn.

The light was dim inside; the smell of corn and manure was pungent. A milk-cow was looking at him inquisitively from her stall. He was frightened she might *moo* and raise the alarm, but her head dropped and she started to chew. He saw a ladder and, still grasping chicken and bread, he climbed to the loft. Apart from thin slivers of light coming from holes in the roof, he was in darkness, but he became aware that he was standing knee-deep in hay. This was obviously the store for the cow's fodder. He stumbled across to the far corner and dropped down. He immediately tore at the chicken with his fingers, stuffing it into his mouth. He had never tasted anything more delicious. With the flesh gone, he sucked the bones. The bread came next.

It was as he finished his last bite that voices and movement sounded from below and lantern-light was suddenly glimmering up through the trapdoor. The creaking of the ladder sounded as heavy weight was put upon it.

Daniel burrowed deeply into the straw, holding his breath and praying that his pounding heartbeat would not give him away. He saw light dancing over the beams and roof above him. Somebody was standing on the ladder and peering into the loft. They did so for what seemed an age, swinging the lantern back and forth. Suddenly it was withdrawn, the ladder creaked again, the light faded and Daniel sighed with relief. The threat seemed to be over — at least for the moment.

With people moving about outside, it would be futile to attempt escape from the barn tonight. He was too weary anyway. He snuggled deeper in the hay and closed his eyes, thankful that he was warm and no longer hungry. The morrow would have to take care of itself. Before long his breathing slowed and he slipped into sleep.

★ ★ ★

Daylight was streaming through the roof's holes when he was kicked to wakefulness. He groaned with fright. A burly man had snatched aside the covering of hay and was looming over him, his heavy-jowled face fierce. Chicken bones were scattered around. With a beefy hand the man grabbed Daniel's collar and dragged him to his feet.

'I think it good to look up here again,' he growled, his accent a guttural German. 'I teach you a lesson, you little thief!'

8

Luiz Prado, the only gang survivor from Mateo's killing spree, ran through the darkness, snatched at by low-swinging fronds from the pines and tripping over his spurs. He ran until his lungs were fit to burst. He trembled with the dread that Mateo might be pursuing him. He had just seen his young brother Ernesto, as well as his other *compadres*, murdered — and but for an intervention by the Saints, he would have been amongst them. They'd all been robbed of the cash that was rightly theirs — or almost rightly.

Now, he slumped against the bole of a tree, and his breath gradually calmed. He strained his ears for any sound of Mateo, but he heard only the normal nightly stirrings of the forest. He had consumed much liquor, had become light-headed, but horror had sobered him.

He himself had gunned down men in plenty, but he considered killing *Yanquis* was acceptable, almost a duty. Killing your *compadres* was the blackest sin.

He had never trusted Mateo, had always been afraid of him. This night was the first time he had lowered his guard, and it had cost him dearly. Foolishly, he had left his cash, pistols and knife with his saddle-bags when he had stepped away to relieve himself. And his horse was still with the others. But as the intensity of his fear subsided, his cunning returned. He concluded that he would not miss his brother unduly, for he was argumentative and petulant. He lamented the loss of the cash more deeply. Now, Mateo had it all. Indeed, Mateo himself would be well worth robbing . . . and killing. Prado tried to suppress his fear of the man, set his mind to scheming.

His first action must be to return to the campsite and pray that Mateo had departed. He would hope to retrieve his weapons, saddle — and his horse, if that was possible.

Accordingly, he rose and stealthily retraced his steps, stopping frequently to listen for Mateo. All he heard was the hoot of an owl, the scurrying of mice and, further away, the yap of a coyote. Through the branches of the trees, he could see the cold white orb of the moon.

Twenty minutes later, he was back at the campsite. The fire was still burning. It had roasted Silvarez, who had fallen into it, a bullet hole in his back. The smell of his scorched flesh tainted the air. The hollow, bathed in light from the flames, presented a ghastly tableau of twisted corpses, including that of Prado's brother, but he paid them no heed. He found his gunbelt and bandolier and strapped them on. He also recovered his sombrero.

Moving cautiously, he located the clearing where the horses had been hobbled. None remained, but he heard them moving about in the trees and he soon found his own *grulla*. He led it back to the hollow, where it scented death and was agitated. He calmed it, got his saddle across its back, fastened the girth and mounted up.

He was sure Mateo would have headed south and that was the direction he took. He rode for two days, keeping to the foothills of the Maroma Mountains, finding cover in pine and oak scrub. He discovered no sign of Mateo; however, he felt certain that the man would be heading for Mexico. On the fourth day, from his high vantage point he spied the southbound trail angling in from the north. His pulse quickened as he spotted movement, but then he relaxed. It was only an armadillo scuttling along . . . but something must have disturbed it. True enough, a lone horseman shortly came into view. There was no mistaking him. It was Mateo.

Luiz Prado knew that the trail curved around low, rocky hills, and any traveller thereon would pass from sight. He also knew that if he climbed over the crest, he would reach a point where he closely overlooked the trail. This would be an ideal place from which to bushwhack his prey.

Moving briskly he spurred the *grulla* upward through the pines and over the crest. Twenty minutes later, having tethered his animal in the brush, he emerged with an excellent, close-up view of the trail. He hunkered down at the mouth of a cave, concealed by a rock buttress. He checked the mechanism of his rifle and waited impatiently. A feral lust to kill had the blood pounding in his ears. He wondered how many bullets it would take to finish Mateo. He licked his lips and thought of the fortune that, the Holy Saints willing, would soon be his.

* * *

Mateo was an old hand at bushwhacking and trailing an enemy. Yesterday, he'd watched birds circling in the sky, sensed the focus of their attention and had known that he was being followed, though by whom he had no idea. He believed that nobody was aware that his saddle-bags bulged with cash; he imagined he had killed his entire gang and he had met no travellers since.

He realized that he was an easy target here on the trail, and an instinctive hunch warned him that danger was imminent, the way ahead being an ideal spot for ambush.

He dismounted and led his roan to the trailside. The animal was agitated as if sensing the proximity of some menace. He tethered it and nose-wrapped it to prevent it sounding off. He unsheathed his rifle, left the trail and climbed into the trees on foot. If his premonitions served him well, he would bushwhack the bushwhacker.

Fifteen minutes later, he grunted with satisfaction, for he could see the back of Luiz Prado. He didn't know how he'd survived the shootings, but he was sure he would die soon.

He had the man's back squarely

within the sights of his rifle but he did not pull the trigger because a strange thing happened.

There was a loud roar. Luiz Prado came to his feet, glanced over his shoulder, his face contorted with terror. A dark, shaggy grizzly bear was rearing up only yards behind him. It had emerged from its cave, its musky smell pervading the air.

Prado raised his rifle, fired and saw dust kick out from the beast's chest. It didn't stop it but enraged it further. It straddled towards him on its hind legs, its fangs bared, saliva dribbling back from its flews, its claws looking like fistfuls of knives. Prado screamed, attempting to run, but he was struck by a monstrous swipe of a paw that ripped his poncho, shirt and flesh beneath, catapulting him forward. He hit the ground hard, the breath thumped from his body. The bear pounced upon him, lying heavily across his hips and legs, crushing him. He was helpless, suffocating in the beast's stench, suspecting his life was ebbing and having no strength to fight on.

Upslope, Mateo aimed his gun, intent on finishing Prado — but again he hesitated, fearing that he might hit the bear. Sensing his presence, the animal paused from biting Prado's shoulder. It cast a glance in the direction of Mateo who decided it would be wise to vacate his present position. Let the brute finish Prado off before it turned its attention on him!

He returned the way he had come, glancing backward to ensure that the bear was not chasing him. At that moment he heard the panicking whinny of Prado's *grulla*. He changed direction, found the animal and freed it from its tether, then he ran on. He reached the roan, removed the nose-wrap, ripped the reins clear of the foliage and mounted up. He moved off straight away.

9

Six months after his shooting, Elmer still felt pain when he put his foot to the ground and he was obliged to rely on a crutch. Nonetheless, he was intensely grateful that he had kept his leg and he frequently thanked God that Doctor Hathaway had been blessed with such medical skill. Each morning he attended Lauren's grave, often bringing flowers, but he was not a man at peace. The old hatreds, lusts for retribution and impatience broiled in him more fiercely than ever.

The Texas Chronicle had reported the strange finding of bodies in the Maroma Mountains; six apparent *bandidos*, all killed by bullets. Assumption was that these were men of Mateo's train-robbing gang, though there was no sign of Mateo himself and no information had emerged as to his whereabouts.

The report fuelled Elmer's intentions to even greater heights. He longed for the day when he could walk unaided, and when he could strike the trail of the monster he wanted dead. Of course, that trail had gone cold. But no man could vanish completely; somebody must know where he was.

★   ★   ★

Otto Schmitt and his wife Olga were German immigrants who, twenty years ago, had come to Texas in search of greater personal freedom and better business opportunities than those afforded in their native Saxony. Through hard work, they had prospered and established the large farm into which Daniel Ramos had now stumbled.

Schmitt was a proud man with a short temper and he could not abide thievery. Grabbing the boy, he half threw him down the loft ladder and descended himself. 'We pass you over to the sheriff, that's what we do, and he can put you in jail — *Ja!*'

Still gripping Daniel, he hastened him across the yard to the scene of the boy's recent crime — the kitchen. There, awaiting them, was Olga, a plump *Frau* in an apron. She had just lifted a skillet of porridge from the stove.

Daniel looked at the woman, expecting to see her scowling and angry at the theft of the chicken and bread. To his surprise she gave him a kindly smile.

'Poor young boy,' she said. 'He's so thin. He must have been starving.'

'Starving or not,' Otto retorted, 'I hand him over to the sheriff. He will teach him not to steal from honest folk. I've heard he whips good-for-nothings.'

Olga shrugged her ample shoulders. 'Well, before you do, let's feed him up. He can have some breakfast.'

Otto grunted his displeasure but let Daniel sit at the table. A moment later a bowl of steaming porridge was placed before him. He'd never had porridge before, but he blew on it and was soon spooning it into his mouth. Next, the woman placed a big sausage in front of him and some bread, which he washed down with strong, black coffee. He could hardly believe his luck.

To her profound regret, Olga Schmitt was a childless woman. She would have loved a son. Now, as she looked at Daniel, her heart warmed.

'Are you running away from the law?' Otto demanded.

'No,' Daniel said. 'I ran away from home. I'm going to join the Texas Rangers at Calico Springs.'

'Texas Rangers, eh?' the farmer said. 'You are a bit young, I think.'

'Perhaps he could stay here, till he is old enough for the Rangers,' Olga suggested.

Otto shook his head stubbornly. '*Nein*,' he said. 'That would not be good.' He scratched his jaw thoughtfully. 'Unless . . .'

'Unless what, Otto?'

The German's mood had softened. 'Unless he worked for his keep. We could do with an extra hand. He'd have to work very hard, mind you.'

'*Ja*, that would be good.'

Daniel had listened with amazement. He had not been consulted, but the prospect of cooked food and maybe a bed to sleep in was too tempting to refuse.

'That *would* be good,' he nodded.

Over the next six months, Daniel worked hard on the farm. He helped the other farm-hand, an elderly German. The tasks were endless, but he loved the life — feeding the animals, cleaning out barns and pens, ploughing burrows and planting crops in the fields, collecting eggs and milking the cows and goats. Wholesome food had him putting on weight, his chest and shoulders broadening.

Otto Schmitt soon became fond of the boy and his industrious nature. He paid Daniel a wage, which he saved, his intention being to purchase a horse. Olga displayed unstinting, homely kindness to him, treating him as a son — but he still cherished the hope of one day becoming a Texas Ranger.

* * *

Elmer had cast aside his crutch a month ago, firstly using a stick and then discarding that. He concentrated on the exercises that Doctor Hathaway had recommended and he found his pain was greatly diminished. Shortly after this, he was in the saddle, pleased that he had lost none of his former skills.

One morning over breakfast, he was scanning through *The Texas Chronicle*, when he noticed a small footnote:

Carlos Viera, the former Mexican bandit, who was severely wounded and captured during a train robbery of a year ago, has recovered sufficiently to be transferred from an infirmary to the penitentiary in

Culver City. He is expected to serve at least ten years.

Elmer's interest had quickened. The bandit might know something of Mateo's whereabouts. He immediately mailed a letter to the prison governor requesting permission to visit Viera. Three weeks later, the response came: *Permission granted.*

Within twenty-four hours he was on a train bound for Culver City.

The penitentiary was a foreboding grey-stone building with a watch-tower, turrets and battlements. Elmer entered through the main entrance, reported to the office and, after authority was granted, was conducted to the prisoners' living quarters. These consisted of small cells on three floors. As he was led along the gangway of the middle floor, inmates grasped their bars and shouted obscenities at him. Ignoring them, he followed the warder to the far end where he was ushered into a cell and the door locked behind him. A stale stench came from the slop-bucket which stood in the corner.

'Fifteen minutes,' the warder stated.

The Mexican, Carlos Viera, who had been sprawled on his pallet, sat up, a look of surprise on his face. His head was clean-shaven and showed an immense scar across its top. Elmer had learned that as well as being shot in the stomach, this man had cracked his skull when falling and been in a coma for weeks. Even now he looked decidedly weak. Viera had probably been complicit in the murder of his wife, and Elmer felt in no mood for salutations. He did not even introduce himself, but got straight to the point.

'You speak English?'

'*Sí, señor* — a li'l.'

'Mateo gunned down all his gang and took the loot from that train robbery all for hisself. I guess he'd have killed you too, if you hadn't been lucky enough to get yourself captured.'

Viera spoke one word: '*Bastardo*!' He

fell back onto his pallet.

Elmer said, 'If you ever wanna get released from this place, you best come clean and tell me where Mateo has his hideaway. Where is he now?'

The Mexican shook his head. 'I no understand.'

'Yes you do,' Elmer persisted. 'Where did Mateo go when he wanted to lay low? Mexico?'

'*Sí*, señor, Mexico.'

'Where in Mexico?'

Again, Viera shook his head, as if bewildered by events.

'You don't owe Mateo anythin',' Elmer said. 'He'd've killed and robbed you if he'd had the chance. He's a mean bastard, a murderer and double-crosser. I mean to kill him myself.'

Viera looked up, surprised. 'You will kill him?'

'That's what I said. That's what he deserves. But I've gotta find him first.'

'You can get me out of this stinking hole?' Viera asked.

'I can put in a good word for you.'

The Mexican gave an exasperated sigh. He spat at the bucket, missed, then he said, 'Go to Amerido, in Mexico. Kill the *bastardo*!'

10

Luiz Prado tried to open his eyes and could not. He was aware of crushing pressure on his chest. Also, an overwhelming stench that was nigh suffocating him — the stench of bear. He attempted to raise his eyelids again; this time he succeeded and light lanced into his eyes, paining him. Where was he? His mind grappled with recollections. He recalled seeing Mateo, and then running from the bear, and after that the agony before he blacked out.

He realized that he was lying beneath the brute. It appeared to be dead. He could hear flies buzzing. He recalled firing a shot, seeing it strike the animal's chest. At the time it had seemed to have little effect, but now he concluded that the bullet must have lodged somewhere vital. The heart maybe? The result had been a delayed action. The bear must have died while it tried to bite and claw him to death. And where was Mateo now?

He struggled to thrust aside the animal and agony shot through every part of his body. Gritting his teeth, he tried again and felt the weight give slightly. He paused, regaining what little strength he had. At the fourth attempt he was able to wriggle out — and now he realized how badly injured he was. His ribs felt broken. He was covered in blood, his clothing ripped to shreds. He tried to straighten up, but this caused him to cry out. He had never known such pain. He thought he might die.

Then Mateo came into his mind. He looked around. Where was the *bastardo?* He had gone. He had left him to the bear. Prado slumped back, ignoring the flies that swarmed around both him and the beast. He lapsed into unconsciousness.

When he regained his senses, the warmth had gone out of the day. Hatred of Mateo enveloped him. He longed to be able to kill him. He knew he must try to move, to drag himself away . . . but to where? In all his life, he had never needed help more. He recalled that he had left his horse tethered way back up the slope in the trees, but he doubted that he had sufficient strength to make the necessary climb. Maybe if he could get down to the trail, some traveller might come along. That seemed to be his best hope.

His progress down the punishing slope was snail-like. He weakened and was reduced to a crawl, dragging his lacerated body along using his elbows and knees, stopping to rest frequently. When, at last, he reached the trailside, night and a cold breeze had come. Wolves were sending their howls up to the pale moon.

Exhausted, he slept.

Black Hawk, a Comanche, found him lying at the trailside just after dawn on the following day. The Indian's ancient face was wrinkled like an old apple. While he was hunting for rabbits, he had stumbled across the dead bear and then the Mexican. Now, he saw that the man's clothing was soaked with blood and through its shreds, mutilations showed. Grandfather Bear must have been very annoyed with this man. At first, Black Hawk thought he had gone to the hunting grounds in the sky, but shortly he saw the rise and fall of his chest.

Black Hawk had always been a loner and three years earlier had been away in the hills when Chief Quanah Parker had led the Comanches onto the reservation in Oklahoma. Ever since, he and the White Eye girl whom he called Little Dove, had pitched their tipi in quiet valleys and the blue-coat soldiers had not troubled them.

Black Hawk sat quietly until the Mexican woke up and groaned with chagrin as he saw the Indian looking at him. Black Hawk lifted the canteen from his shoulder, uncorked it, and touched it to the lips of the man, who took a long gulp.

'I will help you to get up,' Black Hawk said in Spanish.

Surprised at being shown mercy, Prado nodded, and with the Indian's aid he clambered to his feet. He swayed but Black Hawk supported him. He had lost much blood. After a moment, with his arm across the Comanche's shoulders, he took tentative steps forward, wincing at his pain. He had no idea where he was being taken. They went slowly, stopping every few yards. Several times he nearly fell. After a torturous hour, they reached the tipi of Black Hawk where Little Dove was busy scraping the flesh from an antelope hide. She had long black hair and a sensuous body.

She had been kidnapped by the Indians when she was a child. She had soon grown used to the Comanche way of life and Black Hawk had treated her like a granddaughter. She had even attended the reservation school with Comanche children and had learned to understand the tracks White Eyes made across paper. But now, at nineteen, she was restless and capricious, and had secret thoughts that the old man would not have appreciated. Being white, she sometimes ventured into the town of Turtle Rock, traded rabbit skins for supplies and gazed longingly at clothes and jewellery in store windows. She wished she had money with which to purchase them.

Now, Black Hawk quickly explained to the girl in the Comanche tongue how he had found the Mexican. He asked her to clean and treat his wounds. Somewhat reluctantly, she nodded.

While Prado rested down on a pallet within the tipi, she cut away his tattered shirt, gasping as she saw his wounds. She left him and shortly returned with a bowl of water and cloth. With none-too-gentle hands she bathed him and presently she applied antelope fat over the claw and teeth lacerations.

Eventually Prado slept. He dreamed of killing Mateo.

On the following day Black Hawk

gave him an old shirt and pants.

Over the next two weeks he rested a great deal and gradually his strength returned, fortified by rabbit stew. His ribs and wounds still hurt but less than they had previously.

He began to watch Little Dove. Her body was lissom and he yearned to see her naked. One day he asked her for a kiss.

'Kiss you!' she scoffed. 'I don't even know your name.'

'I am Luiz Prado, and women do not refuse me.'

'I do,' she said and turned away.

★　★　★

Next morning, she went to the town of Turtle Rock to get supplies. When she returned, she beckoned Black Hawk out of Prado's earshot.

'In town I saw many posters,' she said. 'They offer much money for the capture of Mexican bandits — dead or alive. I am sure the man we have looked after is a Mexican bandit. We could maybe get the reward for him.'

The old man frowned. 'That is not the Comanche custom,' he said. 'Once a person has been shown hospitality, made welcome in the tipi, it is not the Comanche way to betray him.'

'But I am not Comanche,' the girl said.

The following morning, she again went in to the town.

As he'd begun to recover from his injuries, Luiz Prado had grown uneasy and he felt vulnerable. Each day his desire to kill Mateo increased. Throughout his harrowing experiences, he had somehow retained his gunbelt and pistol and of late had kept them beneath his pallet.

Now, as he rested within the tipi, he heard the girl's voice coming from outside. She had returned from her absence. And then he became aware of the deeper murmur of a man's voice — a stranger's.

With desperate hands, Prado reached

for his pistol, concealing it under his blanket. Almost immediately, the flap of the tipi was drawn back and Sheriff Harlock stepped inside, his gun in his hand.

'I'm arrestin' you on a charge of banditry,' he proclaimed.

Those were the last words he ever spoke. Firing through the blanket, Prado's gun blasted off, the lead cutting clean through the lawman's heart.

11

The boy Daniel Ramos had left the farm with sadness. He had grown fond of the Schmitts; they had been kind to him and he had enjoyed the hard work, yet he now felt it was time to move on, to fulfil his ambition of becoming a Texas Ranger. When he left, Otto gave his hand a long shake and Olga cried, hugged him and kissed his cheek. He had saved his wages and he travelled by stagecoach to Calico Springs, arriving in the early afternoon.

Although the sun was shining and the streets were bustling with normal folk, he still shuddered as he recalled the fearful night when he'd fled from the Mexicans and hidden in a back street.

Today, he had no trouble in finding the office of the Texas Rangers. Steeling himself, he entered to find Captain Bob Justin sitting at his desk. When Justin looked up from his paperwork, Daniel said, 'Good afternoon, señor. I want to be a Texas Ranger.'

Justin smiled. 'It's a hard life, son. You've got to be real tough to stand up to it.'

'I am tough.'

The Ranger eyed him up and down, then said, 'I guess you are. How old are you?

'Sixteen-and-a-half.' It had never entered Daniel's mind to lie.

Justin frowned. 'Too young. Come back when you're eighteen.'

The boy looked utterly crestfallen and Justin took pity on him.

'If you wanted,' he said, 'and if you proved reliable, we could use you to run errands, clean out the stables and a lot of other jobs. The pay won't be great, but if you could do that until you were old enough to join as a grown man, then maybe we could employ you, that's if you qualified.'

Daniel gave him a wide smile and nodded vigorously.

Once again he had been offered work, just at the right moment.

In the days that followed Daniel heard that Elmer Carrington was staying at The Golden Sunrise Guesthouse, and one morning he visited him. To his delight, Elmer welcomed him warmly and set him up with coffee. Daniel expressed genuine sorrow on learning of Lauren's death. For a moment he was quite overcome. Elmer told him it was his intention to kill Mateo. The boy nodded sagely and expressed the opinion that death was too good for the Mexican. Presently he related his own experiences and his ambitions. Elmer listened with interest.

Eventually they parted, wishing each other well.

When Elmer got back from his visit to Culver City, he was excited. At last he might be able to pick up Mateo's trail. Of course there was no guarantee that the Mexican would have gone to the place called Amerido; nor that

Carlos Viera was telling him the truth. But it was the only clue he'd unearthed so far and he had to follow it up.

Before he did so, he penned a letter to the governor of the Culver City Penitentiary explaining that Carlos Viera had given him useful information regarding the notorious Mexican bandit, Mateo. Although he felt no compassion for Viera, Elmer asked that he might be given some consideration. He had, at least, kept his word.

Elmer had never heard of Amerido. He sent away by mail-order for a map of Mexico and when it arrived he studied it and eventually spotted the name in tiny print.

Amerido was a village deep in Mexico. And that was where he intended going.

It took him three days to prepare, arming himself with his Henry .44 Repeater, a Colt pistol, ammunition and a Bowie knife. He purchased a compass and suitable clothing — poncho, shirt, and a sombrero.

On his last evening, Daniel came to him at the guesthouse while he was eating his supper.

'Captain,' he said, 'Captain Justin has told me that you are leaving in the morning, that you are going to Mexico to find Mateo.'

'Sure I am, Daniel,' Elmer responded.

'I have a favour to ask.'

'What favour?'

'A big favour.'

'What is it?'

'I want to come with you!'

Elmer dropped his spoon with a clatter.

After a moment he said, 'You can't. It'll be too dangerous. There ain't no place for a boy in what I'm gonna do.'

'I'm not a boy. I'm almost a grown man. And I hate Mateo real bad. Almost as bad as you. I have bought a pistol to take with me.'

Elmer saw the earnest glint in the boy's eyes. He scratched his jaw. He said, 'If anythin' should happen to you, I'd feel real bad.'

'I'll be very careful, Captain. I promise.'

'But the Rangers won't take kindly to you givin' up your job.'

'Captain Justin has given me leave of absence.'

Elmer took a mouthful of apple pie, then he said, 'All right, you can come, but don't expect a picnic.'

Next morning, Elmer took Daniel to the hardware store and kitted him out with the necessities he would need for the journey. At noon they boarded the stage and thus began a bone-jarring journey on the route known as Polecat Mail. It was to last for three days. The first night they stopped and slept at a way station; on the other nights they travelled on, sleeping on the floor of the coach.

They changed at several towns and finally disembarked at Polka City. Here, they enjoyed a bath at the Tonsorial Parlour, easing the cricks from their bones, stayed overnight at a guesthouse and the following morning bought, from a livery, two sturdy chestnut horses, a pack-mule and tack. Elmer's respect for the boy increased, for he remained cheerful and helpful, never once complaining.

After a final, hearty meal at a restaurant, they continued their journey, crossing into Mexico at a point ten miles south of Polka City. Elmer consulted his map, planning their route through the mountains and then onward into the desert. The compass would prove invaluable. They camped that night in a cave. Having checked for snakes, they lit a mesquite fire and enjoyed their supper despite the gnats that came to pester them. Before dawn, they had saddled up and were moving out, the day breaking before them. Presently, the sun became obscured by cloud and the air turned humid.

The mountains lacked crests, having flat uplands covered with saguaros. The floor of the world seemed cracked open with countless canyons and arroyos which trapped the heat, so that their energy was sapped.

By the time they descended from the mountains, the clouds began to multiply and merge.

'Soon we'll have a big storm,' Daniel opined, and sure enough within minutes thunder rumbled, causing the horses to whinny and rear, and lightning streaked like gunfire through the clouds. The smell of ozone tainted the air and the wind began to rise.

'There's cover over there.' Elmer gestured towards a rock overhang, but the rain came quite suddenly, a bludgeoning downpour with raindrops like bullets splattering on the rock, knocking the berries off junipers, and soaking man and boy. It plastered their shirts to their backs and filled the brims of their sombreros. They reached the sheltering rock too late to save them from a soaking.

For an hour the deluge continued, then trailed off as quickly as it had arrived. Elmer and Daniel looked at each other and suddenly they were laughing because they looked a sorry sight, like a couple of drowned rats. Elmer reckoned it was the first time he had laughed since Lauren had died.

They shook the water from their sombreros, climbed into their soggy saddles and moved on across the puddled ground. It was a half hour later, when they were crossing a shallow wash, that they heard a sound like an approaching freight train. The horses began to rear in alarm.

'What's that?' Daniel cried, his eyes round with fear.

They looked back to see a wall of water, advancing upon them in a crescent shape. It seemed to eat up the ground, coming at incredible speed.

Spurring their panicking animals, they rode up the bank to higher ground, arriving just in time to escape being carried away. They turned to watch the flood surge through the wash — a brown liquid avalanche, dragging trees, branches and debris with it. Two hours passed with the flood unrelenting, then the flow slowed; it gradually dwindled to a gentle stream, passing over bars of quicksand. Swarms of flies came to replace those that had been drowned.

'Best move on,' Elmer said. This was not the first flash flood he had experienced, but it ranked right up there amid the worst.

Again they started off, the animals sometimes hock-deep in mud. The heat and light were fading from the day and they went carefully over the treacherous ground, swatting at the mosquitos that seemed everywhere.

They did not foresee the disaster that awaited them.

They were moving over wet sand, which looked reasonably firm, when suddenly the ground seemed to turn to liquid, and the terrified horses and mule started to sink in what seemed a jelly-like substance. As they struggled frantically, they sank deeper.

Believing that horses and mules would sink more quickly than a man

115

because of their greater weight and the smallness of their feet, Elmer lowered himself from the saddle and eased himself down. He immediately sank ankle-deep in the ooze, but, with tremendous effort, succeeded in drawing his booted feet clear, step by step, until he reached firmer ground. He was thankful that his boots had always been on the tight side.

He turned to see Daniel sliding from his animal, attempting to escape in the same way as he had, but the mud had taken hold of him, was now halfway up to his thighs.

Elmer got as close to the boy as he could without becoming bogged down himself, but their extended hands did not meet.

'Lean forward,' Elmer yelled.

'I am,' Daniel gasped.

'Then try to fall flat on your face.'

Daniel took a deep breath. He reckoned that if such a desperate measure failed, he would be doomed. But with great courage, he did as instructed and Elmer got a hold on his wrists. With a slow, steady pull he began to draw him out, but the quicksand was reluctant to let him go. It gurgled and made gasping noises.

Exerting every ounce of his strength, striving to ignore the pain in his leg, Elmer fought the quicksand for its prize and gradually dragged the boy clear. But his boots remained behind. It was impossible to recover them because the liquid sand oozed into the holes Daniel had left, covering them over, leaving the surface sleek and innocent-looking, just as it had done before they were ensnared.

Daniel sat head down on firm ground, breathing hard and thanking Elmer for rescuing him.

But the problem of the animals remained, and with the light fading, it was going to be difficult to overcome.

12

Elmer came up with a desperate plan. To stand any chance of saving the animals, they needed rope, and the only rope they had was attached to the saddles which were currently on the backs of the trapped mounts.

Elmer pulled off his boots, then his pants and shirt.

'What are you gonna do, Captain?' Daniel gasped anxiously.

'We need rope to get the hosses out,' Elmer responded. 'I'm goin' back into the quicksand. I guess if I spread myself, I won't sink.'

'*Madre mía*!' the boy exclaimed. 'I shall pray for you.'

Elmer grunted his appreciation, waded in to the mud and gently extended himself forward, arms outstretched, slowly pushing with his legs. To his relief he did not sink, but partially floated. Both horses had quieted, appearing resigned to becoming fully submerged.

Elmer reached Daniel's chestnut first. The animal snorted, but he soothed it with a rub of the still-exposed withers. He stretched his arm out and unhooked the rope from the saddle-horn. He uncoiled it, doubled the loop, passed the rope around the horse's neck and knotted it to prevent it sliding. Then, extending the rope as he went, he made it back to firm ground.

The chestnut had not moved, but now as the rope was drawn taut, man and boy heaved with all their weight. At first, all that happened was that the horse extended its neck, whickering with fear. At last, suddenly, it activated its front legs, striving to move forward . . . and slowly, aided by human brawn, it struggled into motion. A further ten minutes saw it on firm ground, shaking itself, its mud-caked body glinting in the moonlight.

The prospect of re-entering the

quicksand was mighty daunting, but Elmer knew he had to do it if the other two animals were to be saved.

Daniel said, 'Let me go, Captain. I saw how you did it.'

Elmer shook his head. 'I'm bigger than you. I can spread my weight more.' With that he waded in again.

Rescuing the second horse was even harder than the first because it had sunk deeper. Pausing frequently, Elmer managed to float his way until he was in position to get the rope around its neck. Thereafter followed another monumental tug-of-war that at times appeared to be failing as the exhausted animal seemed reluctant to help. But at last it was goaded into motion and it, too, was drawn up onto firm ground. Once there, its legs gave out and it rested down on its side, its breath coming in great rasps. Elmer pulled off the saddle and tack and retrieved his Henry Repeater from the scabbard.

Now, there was only the mule to be pulled out. Utterly weary, Elmer waded into the quicksand for the third time. To his dismay, he found the beast had sunk almost up to its withers, weighed down by the packs it was carrying. It was exhausted, its eyes were closed and it seemed already to have given up the ghost. He got the rope around its neck, but soon realized there was no chance of rescuing it, nor the supplies on its back. With a heavy heart, he back-tracked to dry land, retrieved his gun from his belt and checked that it was loaded. He took careful aim and despatched the animal with a single shot to the head.

Daniel shed tears because he had grown fond of the mule.

They bedded down that night feeling crestfallen. Daniel lay awake for hours, watching the moon's mottled face float across the dark sky; he wondered what the future held. Would they find Mateo and give him the punishment he deserved?

Hatred of Mateo made him feel restless. He blamed him for all their misfortunes. Eventually, he rose from his blanket and went to where Elmer's horse was still lying on its side. Its breathing was now steady. Its eyes glinted up at him trustingly. He smoothed its neck and whispered soothing words in to its ear.

He checked his own chestnut, hobbled nearby. It seemed to have recovered from its ordeal. He returned to his bed and rolled into his blanket, aware of Elmer's gentle snore.

He speculated on how he would manage the remaining journey minus his boots. He consoled himself with the thought that he had travelled barefoot before, when he was running from Mateo. Now he was running to him. He slept.

When he awoke, the sun was already rising, burning off the mist from the mountain tops. He climbed up to find Elmer crouching over his prostrate horse. Elmer straightened up and turned, his face gaunt. 'He died during the night,' he said.

Neither of them felt in the mood for breakfast that morning.

When they moved on, they had no wish to burden their remaining mount with a double load, so they took it in turns to ride. They shared their one pair of boots, the walker having the benefit.

Elmer's compass had been lost with the mule, and this would make navigating the desert hard. The map was of little use because the country lacked landmarks. Elmer knew they had to head south and he told Daniel to watch for barrel cacti because they grew pointing south.

The heat became fierce and they urinated in their sombreros to make them cool.

In the afternoon they came to a derelict and deserted copper mine, and were glad to shelter from the heat in one of its shafts. They travelled on when the day became less torrid. That night they camped beneath a tall juniper tree.

After the moon had come, Elmer tried in vain to doze off, but he kept wishing that time would pass more quickly, so that they could find Mateo. Then a doubt occurred to him. Maybe he wasn't in Amerido. Maybe he had left or had never been there.

After the merciless heat of earlier, the night was downright cold. Daniel appeared already to be fast asleep. Suddenly blind instinct jerked Elmer out of his reverie. He glimpsed something moving on the boy's blanketed body, something that caught the moon's glint. Shock caused his heart to miss a beat as stark realization hammered into him — *rattlesnake!*

He was petrified that Daniel would move in his sleep and alarm the snake, causing it to strike. His hand closed over his Colt, but he decided he could not risk a shot for fear of hitting the boy. The snake was now motionless, half coiled, close to Daniel's head, perhaps relishing his warmth. Elmer debated whether to rush at the snake in an attempt to scare it off; the danger was that Daniel would be startled awake and attract the reptile's anger. But maybe it was a chance Elmer had to take. He was tensing his muscles, ready for a leap, when a miracle happened . . . the snake uncoiled itself and moved away, sidewinding in to the darkness.

Elmer exhaled in relief. Daniel suddenly grunted and turned over, pulling the blanket tightly around him. He was none the wiser of the threat he'd just survived.

As they travelled on next morning, following the direction indicated by the barrel cacti, the desert became greener with grama grass and there were occasional stands of willow. At noon, they spied three *vaqueros* driving cattle. Elmer made Daniel dismount and they sheltered in trees, keeping out of sight until the herd had gone by. Later, they passed a village, saw peons working in fields, and a mile or so beyond, a big hacienda, all of which they gave a wide berth. They also steered clear of the well-worn trails that now appeared.

They knew that *Yanquis* were never popular south of the border.

In the evening, a new danger loomed. They had stopped to rest the horse in a gully and Daniel had mounted guard while Elmer was filling their canteens from the stream that flowed through. Suddenly the boy came rushing back from his vantage point. '*Rurales!*' he cried.

Elmer cursed, corked the canteens, and the two of them scrambled back to the gully ridge, crouching down as they scanned the terrain. Riding about a quarter-mile away was a troop of *rurales* with their crossed bandoliers and kepis. Elmer knew that these half-wild *soldados*, so-called enforcers of the law, mostly consisted of killers and bandits released from prison. They had terrorized the *campesinos* of northern Mexico, and were to be avoided at all costs; they had the reputation of being as ruthless as the Apaches. And their hatred of *gringos* was legendary. Thankfully it appeared they were bypassing the gully, moving back along the way Elmer and Daniel had come. That night they sat by their small mesquite fire, warming their toes and feeding on the gila monster lizard that Daniel had trapped. After it was skinned and the meat cooked, it provided a tasty meal.

'How long to Amerido?' Daniel asked, licking his fingers.

'We should make it in a couple o' days,' Elmer said. 'That's if we stay clear of trouble. Just think, in forty-eight hours we could be eatin' goat.'

After feeding, Elmer sat cleaning his Henry Repeater. Daniel looked at it admiringly. 'Maybe when I'm a Ranger,' he said, 'I'll have a gun like that.'

Another day of travel through the blistering heat came and went. It was after they had set up camp in a hollow, with daylight fading, that disaster struck. They were getting their fire lighted when they were startled by the metallic slotting of steel on steel as cocking pieces were levered. They glanced up in alarm to see four heavily moustached *rurales* standing on the rim of the hollow, their rifles pointed at them.

Elmer considered going for his gun, but then realized it would be futile. They'd been completely outwitted. One false move and they'd be riddled with bullets.

The foremost *rurale*, a giant with three chevrons on his arm, gave an evil smile and spat out one venom-filled word: '*Gringos*!'

13

Within minutes, Elmer and Daniel were disarmed and their hands bound behind their backs. At rope's end they were led at a punishing pace by their mounted captors. Presently, as full darkness settled in, they linked up with the main column of *rurales*, which was under the command of a young officer. Elmer heard him called Lieutenant Baca. He viewed the prisoners with pitiless eyes and spat at them. They were given no time to rest as the march was resumed. No allowance was made for weariness. The ground seemed a mass of sand burrs and rocks. Elmer was bare-footed; soon his feet were a bloody mess and his weakened leg throbbed with pain. Daniel strove to stay upright as he was dragged onward. When he stumbled, the giant of a sergeant lashed him with his quirt.

Elmer had no idea where they were being taken but he knew that it would not be a good place. He felt sick with remorse at having brought the boy on this wretched journey.

The night was cold and the frosty moon and stars seemed distant and forbidding.

One brief stop was made and the men dismounted to rest the horses. The prisoners slumped to the ground, but all too soon the sergeant, whose name was Waaz, was lashing at them, cursing and blaspheming, and forcing them to stand. His quirt was made of rawhide and made heavy with lead. As the journey was recommenced, Lieutenant Baca rode at the head of the column, setting a murderous pace and not sparing a glance at the prisoners. At no time was there any attempt to communicate with them.

Stark dawn was painting the distant mountains with the first glimmer of day as they came in sight of a village — a straggle of single-storey, white adobe buildings lining a creek. From the biggest structure a Mexican flag of red, white and green fluttered in the strong breeze. This was clearly a headquarters of the *rurales*. The column speeded up as the horses sensed the nearness of water.

Elmer and Daniel, near dropping by now, realized that some form of rest might lie ahead, and they were goaded into a final effort.

As soon as they arrived amid the adobes, they were assailed by a pack of yapping, rib-thin dogs; Elmer felt sure the animals would have eaten them had they not been bludgeoned away with sabres by the *rurales*. The prisoners were hustled across a courtyard, passing a high adobe wall, aware that they were the centre of attraction for the numerous peons who stood around.

Shortly they found themselves in a tiny room — a cell. There were no windows and no light, apart from that coming through the doorway. A Mexican appeared and unfastened the ropes binding their hands. They dropped onto the dirt floor, working their arms to restore the circulation. A plump woman came in and threw a handful of corn down. She also provided a jug of water. 'For breakfast,' she said.

She and the man withdrew, the door was slammed shut and a key grated in the lock. They were in pitch darkness. They didn't know what to expect, but Elmer feared that they would be tortured, though he didn't reveal his suspicion to Daniel.

'You OK?' he whispered.

'I will be when we escape from this place,' Daniel replied.

'We better make the best of breakfast,' Elmer said, and they both felt about on the ground to pick up the corn. After they had eaten their scant share, they quenched their thirst from the jug. From outside, they could hear the shouts of the *rurales*. It seemed they were doing some sort of drill.

Eventually, they settled back on the ground, trying to sleep, but the heat in the cell was stifling. Presently they heard a scurrying movement across the floor; something bit Daniel's foot and he cried out.

'Rats!' Elmer exclaimed, and the thought was in his mind that when they had scooped up the corn from the floor and stuffed it into their mouths, they might have swallowed a ration of rat droppings. He tried to push the thought away.

He had just dozed off when the rattling of the key in the lock roused him. As the door was flung open, bright sunlight flooded in. Then it was partially blocked out as Sergeant Waaz and two of his men barged through.

The sergeant kicked Elmer and told him to get up. He struggled to his feet and his hands were again tied behind his back. He exchanged a despairing glance with Daniel as he was frog-marched out. He was escorted across the courtyard to the building above which the flag flew.

He was hustled through a doorway.

Upon the door was a sign proclaiming CAPITAINE P. FAURY and he found himself confronted by an officer seated at a desk. He wore a smart grey uniform braided in silver.

It was a mystery how a Frenchman, Pierre Faury, had become a captain and a commandant in the Mexican *rurales*. Perhaps, Elmer concluded, he had come as a government adviser and had subsequently seen a chance of advancement in the country's military. However, it was obvious now that he was in no mood to enlighten his 'guest'.

Faury sprawled back in his chair, bit the top from his cheroot, spat it away and lit up. He had a thin moustache that curled at the ends to a fine point.

Elmer stood before him, his hands tied behind his back. His arms hurt from lack of circulation and his bare feet had left bloody marks on the earth floor. A guard stood on each side of him.

Faury took a long draw on his cheroot, then said, 'Why are you foolish enough to be in this country where Americans are despised, *mon ami?*'

From outside came the crackle of gunfire.

Faury smiled. 'My execution squads are at work,' he said. 'It is my duty to exterminate anybody who violates the law. Tell me why you are 'ere.'

Elmer cleared his throat. 'I came to Mexico to track down the man who murdered my wife.'

''Ave you succeeded?'

'No, but I know where he is.'

The captain's face hardened. 'Every condemned man pleads with me,' he said, 'and I know when they are lying. Now, I am too busy to listen to your pack of merde. You and the boy are spies and you will be shot.'

Elmer bristled with anger. 'We're not spies. But if you won't listen to reason, spare the boy. He is downright innocent. He's Mexican anyway.'

Faury raised his hand impatiently. 'But he's 'elping you, therefore he's as guilty as you. Now enough talk!' he exclaimed. 'You will both die today. Now leave.'

Elmer felt a great surge of regret, not for himself but for Daniel. He should never have brought him.

He was grabbed by a guard who attempted to bundle him from the room, but he stood his ground. 'I'm tellin' you,' he cried. 'Me and the boy came to Mexico to kill Mateo. He raped and strangled my wife and he killed a good many other folks — '

'You say Mateo?' Faury snapped; his interest was suddenly aroused.

The guard was dragging Elmer away, but the captain stopped him.

'Mateo?' he repeated.

'Yes,' Elmer answered, his voice tinged with desperation. 'He's wanted in the States. There's a big reward on his head.'

Faury stubbed out his cheroot. 'He's also wanted in Mexico for crimes south of the border.'

'Then let me kill him,' Elmer said. 'I guess I know where he is.'

'I also know where he is,' the Frenchman explained. 'I've 'ad my agents out. He is living under the name of Eduardo Anza in Amerido.'

'Then why ain't you arrested him?' Elmer asked.

For a long moment Faury didn't answer. He curled the ends of his moustache and assumed a crafty manner. 'I 'aven't arrested him for reasons of my own,' he said mysteriously. 'But I will make you a proposition. I will let you go if you promise to bring me Mateo's 'ead.'

'His head?' Elmer exclaimed.

'*Oui, mon ami.* The 'ead.'

'If you let us go, we will kill Mateo,' Elmer said.

'*Non.* I will not let you *both* go. The boy will stay 'ere. I want Mateo decapitated. If you do not bring me 'is 'ead within, say, two weeks, the boy will die . . . and so will you when we catch you!'

Elmer swallowed hard, trying to give himself time to think. 'One thing I need,' he said.

'What's that?'

'A pair of boots.'

Faury gestured to one of the guards. 'Fetch 'im some boots.' Then he swung back to Elmer. 'Two weeks from today, that's all,' he repeated. 'If you fail, the boy will be executed. I will shoot 'im myself!'

Elmer felt trapped. He didn't like the situation one iota; he didn't trust the Frenchman, but he had no alternative but to nod his compliance.

14

He didn't see Daniel again. Elmer's arms were untied and he was led by the guards to where a cook was tending two huge cauldrons of what appeared to be stew. He was given a bowl of the steaming stuff and scalded his lips as he spooned it down. It was followed by a cup of coffee. He wished he had the means of getting food to Daniel but he was afforded no chance.

A young *rurale* brought him a pair of boots. Another, whom Elmer learned was called Alfredo, was assigned as his escort. Alfredo was about fifty, a tall silent man with blackened teeth and a drooping moustache. He was leading two horses. One was a big sorrel whose reins were handed to Elmer. In broken English Alfredo informed Elmer that he was to guide him to a point close to Amerido where he would give him his weapons and leave him to carry out his assignment. He also warned Elmer that if he tried any tricks, he would kill him. Elmer again wondered why Faury didn't send his own men in to seize Mateo, but could find no answer.

Soon, they were riding out of the village. Elmer was sickened at the prospect of leaving Daniel. He had no idea as to what the future held. All he knew was that he would have to come up with some plan and pray that Faury would keep his word to spare the boy if his conditions were fulfilled. Two weeks would pass rapidly. And now another concern troubled him: supposing Mateo was not in Amerido? He could be anywhere, on either side of the border, and locating him would be as difficult as finding an ant in an anthill.

They rode across the bleak, sun-baked landscape, and because he would no doubt have to make the return journey alone, he tried to memorize the route they were taking. It was not easy, for they were travelling through desert without landmarks apart from saguaro and mesquite, with only a thin ribbon of hills showing in the far distance.

Alfredo retained his silence, keeping in the lead, hardly sparing Elmer a glance. He knew that with the boy hostage, the *gringo* could not afford to attempt escape. The sun burned down upon them but they maintained a steady pace, stopping only rarely for respite.

It was late evening when they reached the hill overlooking Amerido and by then the heat had gone out of the day. Elmer gazed down at the jumble of low adobe structures. There were a few taller buildings including a church with two earthen towers, and a plaza. Beyond, he caught the glint of a river. Everything was rose-coloured in the sunset. Elmer took a deep breath, the ire in him rising. Was Mateo down there?

Alfredo looked at him and nodded, indicating that his task was done and this was as far as he would come. From his saddle-bag, he drew out Elmer's gunbelt, pistols and knife. He dropped them on the ground, as if fearing that if he handed them over directly, they might be turned against him. Then, with a wave of his hand, he turned and would have ridden off had Elmer not called to him, 'I want my rifle too!'

Alfredo swung back, frowning. He grudgingly drew Elmer's Henry Repeater from his scabbard and lowered it down. He'd hoped to keep it but maybe Sergeant Baca would have been displeased if he'd found out. He didn't delay further but spurred away. Soon he was lost amid the saguaros.

Elmer dismounted and retrieved the rifle and the belt, which he buckled on. He climbed back into the saddle and rode down the track that led towards the town. Everything seemed incredibly quiet. Not even a crow stirred in the sky. Again, he pondered on what his best course of action should be. If there was some form of guesthouse, he would book in and then start making inquiries. He wondered if his knife would be sharp enough to decapitate Mateo.

He was approaching the outskirts when he saw the tall wooden board. Big white letters were daubed across it forming three words.

Now he knew why Captain Faury had been unwilling to send his men in to arrest Mateo.

The three words were: *NO ENTRAR — PLAGA!* which translated to a blunt: Keep Out — Plague!

★   ★   ★

After Luiz Prado had gunned down Sheriff Harlock, he rapidly quit the lodge of Black Hawk, leaving the ancient Indian and the girl Little Dove in a state of shock. He left, expressing no thanks to them for reviving him from the dead, and he stole their horse into the bargain. His body was still scarred with lacerations that the bear had inflicted, and the pain from these sharpened his hatred for the man whom he blamed for his suffering and misfortunes — Mateo.

He drove the Comanche's old mare mercilessly, anxious to cover as much distance before the law realized that the sheriff had been murdered. On the third day his mount collapsed from exhaustion. He did not put her out of her misery with a shot to the brain; he was short of ammunition and he left her to expire in her own good time.

He did not intend to remain on foot for long. Also, he was armed with only his pistols and he felt the need for additional weaponry. When he crossed into Mexico and was satisfied that he was safe from pursuit, he remained concealed at the side of a trail while he contemplated further criminal activity.

He waited for two days until a perfect victim came along — a young *vaquero* clad in a fancy jacket, wide sombrero and *chaparreras* decorated with shiny brass buttons. He was astride a proud-looking palomino horse and there was a Springfield rifle in his saddle scabbard.

Prado couldn't trust the accuracy of his pistols at long range, so he walked out from his cover with his hand raised in a friendly gesture.

'*Buenos días, señor,*' he said. 'My horse has thrown me and bolted. I am now on foot. How far is it to the town?'

The *vaquero* eyed him, then smiled. 'Six miles,' he said. 'It's a long way to walk on a hot day. Do you want me to help you find your horse?'

'*Sí, señor.* That would be most kind.'

'In which direction did he go?'

Prado pointed vaguely to the hills behind him.

'Jump up behind me,' the *vaquero* suggested.

Prado nodded, accepted the man's helping hand and swung up onto the palomino's back. Once astride, he unsheathed his pistol, pressed the muzzle against his benefactor's spine and pulled the trigger. The detonation bludgeoned his ears.

The *vaquero* uttered no cry, but plunged from the saddle to the ground, the back of his jacket displaying a large, powder-blackened hole.

Prado struggled to control the panicking palomino. It took him several minutes before he was calmed. He eventually dismounted, led the animal to the side of the trail and tethered him.

He satisfied himself that the *vaquero* was dead, then dragged the body off the trail, hiding it in the bushes in case somebody else came along. The man was wearing a bandolier; slotted into it were a few bullets for the rifle, but unfortunately not many. Prado unbuckled the bandolier. He checked the man's pockets and found only a few pesos. From the corpse, he pulled off the clothing, boots and fitted spurs and replaced his tattered own. Sadly, the jacket was ruined with the gaping hole burned in its back.

Having assured himself that there was nothing else worth thieving, he returned to the palomino, untethered him and mounted, spurring forward. He patted the butt of the Springfield rifle and grinned, well pleased with the day's work. Now he must concentrate on his aim: to kill Mateo.

15

When Mateo had arrived in the sleepy little town of Amerido, he had assumed his real name: Eduardo Anza. Nobody knew that when he was away on so-called 'business' he indulged in banditry. He returned to the comfortable house he owned. Here, he employed as housekeeper the widow Señora Catalina Torrejon. For reasons known only to herself, she was fond of Mateo, or Eddy as she called him. She fussed over him, cooked tasty meals and even provided bedroom comforts when he was so inclined.

For his own part, Mateo, who was now a rich man, was content to enjoy the luxuries he could afford. At least for the time being. He gambled with the local gentry, showing an incredible lucky streak. He enjoyed his trips to the nearby town of Vallejo where there was excellent cock-fighting to bet on. In Amerido, he frequented the bordello and cantina, and even spent evenings with the padre, sipping his fine burgundy wine. Often he attended Mass on the Sabbath, undertaking confessions, though he only recounted minor sins committed since his return.

It is debatable for how long this life would have satisfied him, because sometimes at night he dreamed of the old days, of riding roughshod over *gringos*, of lifting large amounts of loot. Maybe that would be for the future.

Matters continued in an agreeable fashion for a year, but then one evening, returning from a cock-fight in Vallejo, the bullet came. He plunged from the back of his sorrel, landing in the thick cover of mesquite.

★　★　★

Luiz Prado cursed. For days he had dreamed of this sort of opportunity coming his way. The unmistakable figure of Mateo riding alone had made an excellent target, albeit a little further off than he would have chosen. Nonetheless, he had had him dead central in his sights It was as he was about to pull the trigger that the pressure of the rifle butt in his shoulder found a tender spot — a laceration that the bear's claws had left. The slightest of flinches caused his aim to move fractionally away from the intended target of Mateo's chest — but he believed he might have hit him in the head. He could not be sure. Mateo had dropped from his saddle like a sack of grain and disappeared into the brush, his horse galloping on. He might be dead.

But long ago Prado had reached the conclusion that Mateo was as crafty as sin, and he had the sort of luck that only a devil could boast.

Prado strained his eyes, scrutinizing the spot where Mateo had disappeared, but he could determine nothing. He was reluctant to quit his own cover, expose himself, and go to investigate. He gazed at the sky. The light was fading to twilight grey. Within an hour or so night would deepen. He would wait for darkness, then make his way down and hopefully find Mateo's corpse. The prospect excited him, though doubt still warned him that he would have to apply the utmost caution.

Time slipped away. Bats flitted above his head. His eyes ached with his constant surveillance of the mesquite, until at last dusk gave way to darkness. He made his move before the moon and stars came out. He crept down the slope with his Remington at the ready. He wished he had more ammunition. It grieved him that he had no money to purchase bullets, while Mateo had kept all the fortune they'd jointly stolen for himself. But now Mateo was dead . . . maybe.

He crossed the trail, reached the tangled mesquite. It loomed before him, the branches reaching out like ghostly claws. He forced his way into the thicket. All at once there was a great scurrying of movement before him and he nearly died of shock as the large black shape of a bird rose skyward, its wings beating the air like whipcord. He crouched down, his breath heaving. He was about to continue his search, when his hand touched something soft. He picked it up; it was a sombrero. A strange compulsion had him running his fingers around its brim, finding the hole where the bullet had passed through. He wept tears of chagrin, knowing that somehow Mateo had eluded him in the darkness.

★ ★ ★

For days after his escape, Mateo remained in the town, reluctant to venture out and present himself as a target. He tried to determine who his assailant had been, giving no thought to Luiz Prado whom he believed had been killed by the bear. He knew he had many enemies, men who wanted him dead, but most of these were from north of the border. He decided to lie low for a while.

But then the plague hit Amerido and everything changed. It started with a few of the poorest peons falling foul of the disease and dying. When the town's doctor and mayor were smitten and passed away, matters became serious. Shortly deaths were commonplace amongst not only the impoverished, but the rich as well.

Mateo remained indoors with the blinds drawn, and Señora Torrejon boiled water furiously to kill infection. But she was obliged to leave the house on occasions to replenish supplies, and maybe that was when she caught the bug.

She was afflicted with malaise, pains in the limbs, headache and diarrhoea, together with a raging temperature. After five days, she developed a rash of red spots.

She lay in bed, twisting and turning.

She kept crying out for him ...
'Eddy ... Eddy,' but it got on Mateo's
nerves and he tried to ignore her. He
chose not to frequent her room any
more than necessary, for it smelt and he
did not wish to become infected. He
supplied water, but he was thankful she
refused food.

She finally settled into a low,
muttering delirium, and eventually, she
died.

With absolute distaste, Mateo removed
her body to the street for collection by
the cart that gathered corpses.

He himself felt ill, but at first he put
it down to his imagination. He checked
himself over and over for red spots but
found none. Even so, he took to his
bed, inflicted by a shivering.

He lay for many hours, sometimes
hearing women wailing in the streets
outside as the disease claimed more
victims. When he did lapse in to sleep a
strange thing happened, for he was
beset with dreams that were different
from any he'd previously experienced.

He saw again the contorted faces of people he'd tortured — men, women and children. He saw again the twisting bodies of those he had gunned down, or set afire or raped. He saw again the face of the Carrington woman as he strangled her. Their screams were ringing in his ears — their pleas for mercy. And he had spat at them and laughed. And in his dream, he now felt his own vulnerability because everything seemed to change. All his victims had risen from the dead, were chasing him, shrieking their hatred at him. He was running, stumbling and finally he fell.

He would wake in a lathering sweat, shouting his own pleas, knowing that no mercy would come. It was in such a moment that he determined to make amends for all his sins. He would go to the padre, confess everything, and he would beg forgiveness no matter how many 'Hail Marys' he was obliged to recite.

As he rose from his bed and pulled

on his clothing, a realization came upon him. He had no red spots and he was no longer shivering. In fact he concluded that he was not, after all, afflicted by the disease.

He left his house and passed along deserted streets, crossing the plaza. He was glad that the cart had recently done its rounds, clearing away the dead. He reached the padre's episcopal residence and stepped into the courtyard with its potted oleander trees. Everywhere was very quiet. Near the main door, the padre's surrey with its fringed canopy and brass lamps was drawn up, but it lacked a horse within its shafts.

He pulled on the big bell that hung at the main entrance. Twice he rang. There was no response. Gingerly, he turned the doorknob and stepped inside. No one was about, not even the major-domo.

'Father Almundo,' he called. He waited but there was only silence. He knew the padre's study-cum-bedroom was on the first floor. He mounted the narrow stairway and went along the landing. A knock on the door at the far end brought no answer, so he entered. The room was in semi-darkness, but the familiar smell of sickness hung on the air. He went to the window, raised the blind, allowing light to flood in. And then he saw Father Almundo.

The priest was lying on his bed, his face a mass of red spots. Mateo knew that he would be taking no confessions today or ever again. He was dead, his features twisted in anguish. Was meeting his maker such a torment?

Mateo was about to back out of the room, when he noticed the padre's vestments hanging from the picture rail — cassock with crimson piping, violet vest, coat and britches. An idea came to him, humility leaving him to be replaced by the old craftiness.

He quickly stripped off his own soiled clothing and pulled on that of the priest, together with the rectangular clerical cap. He drew a scarf across his face as a protection from infection, went down the stairs and back out into the courtyard.

He knew that the mare would be in the little stable at the side. He went to this and led the animal from her stall. Within five minutes, he had her between the shafts of the surrey.

16

Daniel was distraught when Elmer did not return after he was escorted out. He had heard shots from outside and wondered if he had been executed. The thought filled him with depression. He had no way of telling what had happened. For long, dreary hours he remained in the small cell, the monotony broken only by a *rurale* bringing him meagre food and water and emptying his slop bucket. He asked the man questions: What has happened to Elmer? What will happen to me? Why am I being kept alive? But the man did not answer and Daniel concluded that he was dumb.

At last Sergeant Waaz and another *rurale* appeared and ordered him to his feet. He scrambled up and his hands were immediately bound behind his back. He was then marched out into the sunlight — the fear that he was about to be shot had his heart pounding. But he was hustled past the grim execution wall to the office of Captain Faury. He stood before him just as Elmer had a few days earlier. This time the captain had his feet on his desk.

'You are Mexican,' Faury said, 'so why were you 'elping the *gringos?*'

Daniel clamped back on his jangling nerves, forced his voice to sound steady. 'I was going to join the Texas Rangers.'

Faury contrived a wry grin. 'Why should a good Mexican boy want to join the *Americanos?*'

'My Mexican parents were killed by Comanches,' Daniel said. 'I was brought up by an American.'

Faury bit the end from his cheroot and spat it out. 'You are a strong lad. You should not have wasted your time wanting to join the Texas Rangers. It grieves me that I must now shoot you.'

Daniel stemmed his sudden surge of fear. 'What happened to my *compadre,* Captain Carrington?'

'He will not trouble you any more,' Faury said. He smiled to himself. The American would never return with Mateo's head within two weeks, of that he felt sure. 'I do not think we will keep you waiting,' he said. 'That would be unfair. You must be executed promptly.' He addressed the sergeant who gripped Daniel's arm. 'Take 'im out,' he commanded. 'I said I would shoot 'im myself. It will be a pleasure. Have 'im at the wall in one hour. I 'ave some paperwork to complete first.'

Sergeant Waaz said, '*Sí, Capitaine*,' and Daniel was dragged out. Five minutes later he was back in his cell with the door locked, his arms still bound. He collapsed onto the dirt floor and wept. The heat seemed more suffocating than ever. He tried to tell himself that he wasn't afraid to die — but he was. And there was something else: their mission had ended in abject failure. He felt guilty. He believed that he had dragged all this misfortune onto Elmer and now there was no way he could redeem himself.

He felt he was battling a torrent as he struggled to prevent time from passing. He yearned to be free, to be alongside Elmer, who had been a good friend. His head and arms ached. He wondered what it would be like to be dead. Rats came to scurry about him in the darkness, and he felt almost in communion with them as they shared with him the last moments of his life. He wanted to make the most of every minute, but there was nothing he could do.

Eventually he gave up, lapsed into a stupor. He was roused from it when the key rattled in the door and he knew his time had come. It was Sergeant Waaz again; he hooked him beneath the armpit with his great paw and hoisted him up as if he had no weight. Another *rurale* placed a blindfold over his eyes. He was guided like a blind man to the outside and forced along at a pace far quicker than he would have chosen. The sun's heat felt as if it was broiling his brains. He stumbled but was held up. He sensed that many people were standing around, watching.

When they stopped, and Sergeant Waaz released his arm, he knew he had arrived at the wall.

'Where is the *capitaine*?' somebody inquired.

'He is coming now!'

There was a burble of excited voices. These were people who must have seen many executions, yet this one seemed to arouse particular interest.

He heard the sergeant say, 'All is ready, *Capitaine*.'

Faury's French voice came, though Daniel couldn't hear the exact words.

The metallic sound of a heavy pistol being cocked sounded. He was trembling, he couldn't help it.

Faury spoke again, and this time his voice came loud and clear. '*Adieu, mon ami*. This will teach you not to spy for the Americans.'

There was a lengthy pause, seconds that seemed like hours . . . then the gun exploded with a deafening 'crack!'

Daniel collapsed like a poleaxed calf. He lay on the baking earth, and as his ears recovered from the gun's blast, he was aware of laughter. He wondered if he was in heaven, but immediately knew he wasn't because dirt had ploughed into his mouth. He spat it out. The laughter was growing louder, not from one person but from many. He heard the crunch of boots beside him and the blindfold was suddenly tugged from his head. He was blinking in bright sunlight.

Captain Faury was standing over him, the pistol in his hand. He could hardly contain himself for laughing. 'Why did you fall down?' he asked.

Daniel forced himself into a sitting position. 'That is what people do when they are shot,' he mumbled.

'But you were not shot,' Faury said. 'My pistol fired only a blank. It was a test of your courage.'

Anger flared in Daniel's young eyes, but he held his tongue.

'I have been thinking,' the captain said. 'I think you are too good for the Texas Rangers. I will give you two options. The first is that you join the *rurales*. The second is that you will die, and next time I will not use a blank.'

Daniel knew he had no choice. After a moment he said, 'I will join the *rurales*.'

Faury nodded with satisfaction. 'I must warn you. If you desert or betray the trust I will place in you, we will catch you and you will die the most hideous death imaginable.'

Daniel nodded.

The captain placed his hand on Daniel's shoulder, like a kindly father, and said. 'There is one more thing I must tell you. Before you join us, there is a test you must take. We need to make sure you are not a coward. It is quite good fun.'

'What test?' Daniel murmured. He felt he was beyond caring. Let them do what they liked to him.

'You must spend a night in the

snakepit,' Faury said. He lifted his hand from the boy's shoulder, laughed again as a ripple of applause came from the onlookers.

★ ★ ★

Luiz Prado had just finished eating a raw lizard. It wasn't very wholesome, but it was all he had. Ever since he had been thwarted in his attempt to kill Mateo, he had camped, hidden in the mesquite brush overlooking Amerido. Once, he had ventured in close to the town but had turned back on seeing the sign proclaiming the plague. He wondered if Mateo would catch the disease and die a grisly death. He hoped not. He still craved to kill Mateo himself and decapitate him. He would then be able to present his head to the Mexican authorities and claim any reward on offer and also satisfy his lust for revenge. One thing that grieved him currently, however, was his lack of ammunition for his rifle and handgun.

He had used both in hunting game.

It was evening when a movement attracted his attention. A small, canopied surrey, pulled by a single horse, had left the town and was coming up the trail. As it drew closer, he saw that driving it was a figure in the unmistakable garb of a padre, complete with rectangular clerical cap.

Prado was desperate and frustrated. He had no wish to violate a man of the cloth; on the other hand, the padre might have a fat purse in his pocket. He decided against killing him and thus displeasing the Saints. Instead, he would simply relieve him of his money, which would only count as a small sin.

He stepped onto the trail, ahead of the approaching surrey, raising his hand in the friendly gesture he had used just before he had killed the *vaquero*.

The surrey pulled to a halt.

'*Buenos días*, Father,' he called. 'My horse threw me and I am on foot. I fear to go into Amerido because of the plague. Can I beg a ride with you?'

He gazed up at the padre. A scarf was drawn across, concealing his face, but there was something familiar about the eyes. At the same instant that Prado recognized this man he was hunting, Mateo snatched a pistol from beneath his cassock. Simultaneously, Prado threw himself to the side, snatching out his own gun. Both men fired at the same time, but neither bullet found its mark. However, the blast was enough to have the horse rearing in panic, nearly tipping over the surrey and as its forelegs returned to the ground, the animal charged off at a crazy gallop.

Mateo fought desperately to retain his seat, but still managed to get off another shot. Again it went wide. Prado took a more measured aim. However, his hand was shaking and the bullet missed the hunched body on the surrey seat and sped on to hit the panicking horse, which plunged to the ground, dragging the wagon onto its side in the process.

Prado had a brief glimpse of Mateo

falling clear, but he didn't linger. He ran headlong down the hill, kicking his way through the brush in giant strides. Perhaps Mateo had been badly injured in the fall; perhaps he was even dead. But Prado knew he had only one shot left in his own gun and, if Mateo had survived, he would stand little chance if it came to a shoot-out. Now all he could do was cover as much distance as possible because if further shots came his way they might not be so inaccurate.

Ten minutes later, he drew up, his breath heaving, and gazed back up the hill. He could see the canopy of the stricken surrey, even the bulk of the horse lying motionless — but there was no sign of Mateo. He shuddered.

He hurried on towards the town. He daren't return to his campsite and horse. Not with a nigh-empty gun. Not with Mateo lurking. But as he continued the confidence grew in him that Mateo was out of the reckoning, that he had succumbed to the fall. Gradually his fear dissipated. An idea took root in his mind. He would chance his luck with the plague, go in to Amerido, find Mateo's house. And even more importantly, find the hoard of unexpended cash that was surely there.

17

Elmer was stunned when he saw the sign proclaiming the plague. No wonder everything appeared so silent, and no wonder Captain Faury had set him free to attempt this crazy mission. He looked ahead at the jumble of buildings, all hazed now as dusk settled in. Many questions pounded at his mind: Was Mateo in the stricken town? Had he succumbed to the disease? If he, himself, didn't return to the *rurales'* headquarters within two weeks, would Faury really kill Daniel? If he ventured in to Amerido, would he fall foul of the plague? What hope would there be for Daniel then? He pondered long and hard and finally reached a decision. It seemed he had little option but to enter the town and chance his luck. But firstly he would wait for darkness.

He dismounted to rest the sorrel. He

was desperately hungry, but he had no food. However, he had been given a canteen, which still contained some water. He poured a little into his sombrero and presented it to his animal to suck up. He finished the rest himself.

He hunkered down and wondered about Daniel. Had he been fed? Was he still surviving the cramped, rat-infested conditions of his cell?

So many questions made him dizzy, and the old pain in his leg still throbbed. The night seemed to take an eternity to come, but eventually he considered it gloomy enough to conceal his approach. He climbed into his saddle and urged his mount along the deserted trail towards the town. He went slowly, having no idea what he would do when he got there.

When he reached the outlying adobes, there were no lights or signs of life. Surely not everybody was dead!

He arrived at the head of the main street and saw the glimmer of candle-light showing from a window. His horse plodded on for some twenty yards, the clip of his hoofs on the cobbles sounding loud. Suddenly the moon drifted out from behind a cloud, a cold, white orb that cast grotesque shadows.

Off to his left he saw a faint light glowing from an adobe. Above its doorway he could just make out the words PABLO'S CANTINA. He pulled up and dismounted. He fastened his reins to a hitching post by a water trough, stepped onto the veranda and tried the door. It opened easily and he entered. On first glance, the place seemed deserted, but a lighted candle was set on one of the tables. It was burned halfway down.

He called, '*Hola!*' and after a moment there was a shuffling sound and a gaunt figure in an apron appeared from a back room. Elmer gasped. The man was a walking skeleton. His bones jutted out; the flesh seemed to hang loose from his bean-stick arms; his eyes glowed like burning coals. This must be Pablo, Elmer thought.

'*Señor*,' his voice was like the faint rasp of a saw, 'you should not come here. It is a place of . . . death.'

'I need food,' Elmer said.

Pablo started to protest, then gave up as if it was too much effort. 'I have very little,' he said. He moved out into the back room. Elmer sat on a chair and waited. From somewhere outside he could hear a woman sobbing with grief.

Presently the man returned with a chunk of mesquite bread and some corn tortillas on a plate, a jug of water and a cup. The food was stale; mould showed on the bread but Elmer was in no mood to be choosy and he rapidly devoured it. He was thirsty. He was tempted with the water. He poured some into the cup, raised it to his lips, but then put it back down on the table. He had heard that the plague was spread through water. Pablo stood watching him.

'You are *gringo*,' he stated in his rasping voice. 'You will die if you stay in this place. Why you come here?'

'I am here to see an old acquaintance,' Elmer replied. 'I don't know if he is still alive. His name is Mateo. Do you know him?'

Pablo looked puzzled. He shook his skull-like head. 'Nobody of that name in Amerido.'

Elmer felt perplexed. Was he on a fool's errand?

Somehow, he had retained some coins in his pocket. He drew a few out and placed them on the table. They were sufficient to pay for his meal and more besides. All at once he recalled what Captain Faury had told him. *He is living under the name of Eduardo Anza.*

'Do you know Eduardo Anza?' he asked, and saw Pablo's eyes widen slightly.

'No, *señor*. I know nothing.'

Elmer threw down some more coins. He was sure the man was lying.

'I don't want money,' Pablo said. 'I want what the Lord has taken from me — my woman and child.' And then he added, 'I'm dying, anyway. I have spots.'

'I'm sorry,' Elmer said, 'but I need to find the truth.' He placed the remaining coinage on the table. It was a generous sum. 'Eduardo Anza,' he repeated.

Pablo gazed at the money. He licked his lips.

'Where does he live?' Elmer persisted.

Pablo hesitated for a long moment, then he relented. He reached out with his skinny hands and scooped up the coins. 'Biggest house down the street, on the other side,' he said.

Elmer came to his feet, expressed his thanks and wished Pablo God's blessing. He left the cantina, but as he did so Pablo followed him to the door. '*Señor*,' he called.

Elmer halted and looked back.

'Maybe I should tell you,' Pablo said. 'You are the second man to ask the same question tonight.

'You mean . . . ?'

'*Sí*. A half-hour ago. Another man, a

stranger, a *vaquero*. I think he is an *hombre malo* — a bad man. He asked where Eduardo Anza lives.'

Elmer grunted with surprise. He touched the brim of his hat in recognition of the man's help.

He left his big sorrel hitched to the post and moved down the deserted street, keeping to the shadows and subduing the sound of his footfalls. There was no mistaking Mateo's house when he reached it — one of the few with a second storey. Treading quietly, he climbed onto the veranda and stood before the main door. No light showed through the windows. Who was the other man, and what business did he have with Mateo? He wondered if Mateo was inside, maybe asleep . . . or maybe dead from the disease.

When he touched the brass knob, he realized that the door was slightly ajar. Drawing his pistol, he eased it open and stepped inside. He was in a room that was dark, the blinds drawn. The air was tainted with a sickly staleness. He stood silently, straining his ears for sound. He heard nothing. Feeling his way, he crept to the two other downstairs rooms as well as the kitchen and found no sign of life. He tackled the staircase, climbing slowly, keeping to the side to prevent it creaking. In the first bedroom the blinds were raised, allowing the moon to shine in. There was an unmade bed but no other evidence of human habitation.

It was as he returned to the landing, moved along to the doorway of the second bedroom, that a pungent scent touched his nostrils . . . unwashed body and stale sweat! He waited, holding his breath, his heart suddenly thumping. *Somebody was on the other side of the door.*

Impatience flared in him. He lunged, throwing his body against the half-open door, slamming it back with great force. Somebody yelled out and a gun blasted off — a deafening roar and a bright flash in the confinement of the room.

The bullet smashed the far window, splintering the glass.

Elmer flailed with his arms, lost his hold on his pistol and found himself grappling with a shadowy figure. At first he thought it must be Mateo, but as they struggled he realized that was not the case. His opponent was a bigger man, and his hands were clawing for Elmer's throat. He brought his knee up to the man's groin and heard him yell with pain as he was thrown back, crashing against the metal bedstead in the process.

Elmer went after him but couldn't locate him in the darkness. However, his opponent found him with a vicious kick in the side. Ignoring the pain, Elmer grabbed his leg and twisted it, throwing the man down. He was on him like a catamount, ramming hard with fists and knees, pressing his weight down onto his body, ramming his head into his face.

His opponent was suddenly screaming with pain, screaming for mercy.

Elmer relented slightly, still pinning the man beneath him. Both were slippery with sweat; they lay still, their breath coming in heaving gasps. Elmer knew that his opponent must be the *mal hombre* Pablo had mentioned. He also sensed that his own strength alone had not vanquished him . . . maybe he had another injury.

'*Señor*,' the Mexican hissed through clenched teeth, 'I can fight no more. I am badly hurt. I give in to you.'

'Who are you?' Elmer demanded.

'I am Luiz Prado. And I have . . . killed Mateo.'

'Killed him!' Elmer gasped.

'*Sí*. He was disguised as a priest, trying to escape this town. But he didn't fool me.'

'So you shot him?'

Prado grunted in assent. 'I think maybe he have cash on him . . . but he had nothing, so I come to his house, try to find where he had hidden it. Then you appear . . . '

Elmer tried to absorb what Prado

had said. He somehow couldn't believe that Mateo was dead. He suspected that the man was lying, but he had no way of proving it, not yet.

18

Daniel gazed down into the pit. He was standing on its rim. His boots had been removed. His hands were no longer tied. A number of *rurales* were watching as Sergeant Waaz lowered a rope ladder over the side. The pit was some ten feet deep and fifteen feet across. Its sides were sheer — plastered smooth with adobe clay. There was neither hand- nor foothold.

It was dusk and although Daniel peered hard he could see no snakes in the shadowed depths. He suspected that they were hiding beneath the scattered rocks.

The sergeant gestured for him to climb down. For a second, Daniel considered making a run for it, to keep going until he was clear of this awful place, but when he glanced into the faces of the surrounding *rurales*, he knew it would be futile.

He swallowed hard and began his descent. It was then that he heard the loud buzzing sound from below, and he paused on the ladder, feeling sweat trickling down the nape of his neck. He had always feared rattlesnakes more than any other.

'Go on! Go on!' Sergeant Waaz snarled. 'Or I take the ladder away and you will fall.'

Daniel inched his way downward until his bare feet stepped onto the rocky floor of the pit and immediately the ladder was drawn up from his grasp. It was now quite gloomy. The buzzing had ceased, but he imagined that the air was pungent with the smell of snakes.

He crouched, making himself as small as possible. He was afraid that any movement would attract a strike. He glanced up, expecting to see faces staring down at him from above, but there were none. He felt deserted by humankind, left to die with only the companionship of rattlers.

He strained his ears, listening for slithery movement over rocks. He wondered how close they were. Perhaps some were coiled inches from where he cowered; perhaps they sensed the heat of his body.

Trying to grip his jangling nerves, he consoled himself with the thought that he had survived the first minutes of his ordeal. Maybe there was only one snake in the pit. Maybe it had gone to sleep. His hand closed over a small rock. He clutched it to him. It was, at least, a weapon of sorts.

Presently the moon drifted into view above the rim of the pit. Around him, everything was bathed in silver light and stark, black shadows. Then he saw the snake coiled so close that his breath was snatched away. It was heavy-bodied, black-tailed, its diamond-shaped blotches blending with the ground. It raised its triangular head; its rattle was erect. This time the buzz was deafening.

In panic, Daniel erupted into life,

slamming the rock with all his might into the reptile's head. It fell back. He was on it immediately, pinning its head to the ground with the rock, pressing with all his crushing weight. The snake threshed for an age; Daniel's arms ached with the effort of holding it. At last it lay still, its head nigh severed, and he shifted clear of it, panting and sweating. He returned to his original position, hunkering down. He listened for more buzzing, and sure enough he heard it, but this time from further away. However, his hope that there was only a single snake in the pit was false.

Presently the snakes quieted and the moon and stars became obscured by cloud, so that he was in total darkness. He knew that this would make no difference to the rattlers, for their sight was minimal, relying on their bodies to sense the warmth from other creatures. He remained as still as possible. If there were snakes nearby he didn't want to disturb them. He knew there was nothing else he could do but pray and this he did. Minutes lengthened into hours. He tried to doze, but suddenly he jerked to wakefulness. He felt something crawling over his foot.

He looked down and saw a big scorpion; it had pincers like a lobster and its body glinted with hairs. He jerked it away and crushed it with his rock.

Sometimes his ears seemed to play tricks on him and he heard again the deadly buzzing sound. Maybe he did or maybe he did not; he could not be sure. He wondered if Faury would keep his word and allow him out of the pit once the night was over. Or was it a trick, and he would be left here to die — if not from snakebite, from starvation?

At last he slept, fitfully at first and then more deeply. When he awoke a grey light was showing in the circle of sky that was within his vision. Gradually it filtered down into the pit. He gazed around for snakes but saw none. They must be hiding in the crevices. Shortly, he heard sounds coming from the village — the crowing of a cockerel, the clinking of breakfast pots, the murmur of voices, the barking of dogs.

Again, doubts assailed him. Was the plan to forget about him, to leave him to face a gruesome death?

An hour later, he looked up to see Waaz's face leering down at him. The sergeant tossed Daniel's boots into the pit, well away from the boy. He was laughing loudly. Daniel was obliged to cross amid the rocks, fearful that he might step on a snake, but he made it safely to his boots and pulled them on.

Meanwhile Waaz had dropped the rope ladder into the pit.

'Hurry up,' he called, 'unless you like it so much down there you want to stay!'

Daniel grabbed the ladder and, on stiff legs, climbed upwards.

⋆　⋆　⋆

A young *rurale* was assigned to watch over him. He was allowed to eat breakfast of eggs, tortillas and corn-bread, washed down with coffee. After this he was marched over to the commandant's office. Captain Faury appeared to be in good humour. He congratulated Daniel on surviving his night in the snakepit and proving his courage.

'Per'aps you make a good *rurale*,' he smiled, smoothing the points of his moustache. 'You will get your uniform when you 'ave earned it, not yet. I 'ave decided that you will go on a patrol with Lieutenant Baca. You must be good and obey orders. I 'ave told 'im that if you misbehave in the slightest way, 'e is to whip you and bring you back to me. I will make sure you have a slow death, make you wish you 'ad never been born. But afterwards, I will show you mercy and decapitate you. You understand?'

Daniel said, '*Sí, Capitaine,*' But already his mind was dwelling on the prospect of escape.

In the afternoon, a column of a

dozen mounted *rurales*, plus Daniel, set out on a patrol. They were all heavily armed with sabres, carbines and pistols, with the exception of Daniel, who was given no weapons. He had been supplied with a strong sorrel horse and he was positioned in the centre of the line in the charge of the veteran *rurale* called Alfredo.

The hours dragged by as they rode in a wide circle through searing heat. They searched the desert country for tracks of *bandidos* or Apaches, but they found none. They called at three villages where the peons showed them no hospitality and gazed at them with hateful eyes.

Lieutenant Baca frequently checked on Daniel, who watched out for any opportunity of escaping, particularly when they stopped for respite, but Alfredo remained close, even pissing alongside him, and no chance presented itself. He decided he would have to wait for another day.

He was weary when, that night, they

returned from the patrol. He was glad to eat a hearty supper and retire to the cot he was allotted. For a while he thought of Elmer, wondering what had happened to him, but eventually he slipped into a sound sleep.

Next day he was set to work, peeling potatoes. He saw nothing of Captain Faury and Lieutenant Baca, though Sergeant Waaz watched him for a while and conversed with the cook.

On the third day of his 'enlistment', he was assigned to another patrol, which was commanded by Sergeant Waaz. Again, he was given no weapons — and a boyish *rurale*, Pedro, was put in charge of him. Once again hours of hard riding took them in a wide circle, following a different route from that of the previous patrol. This time they were drenched by a heavy summer storm. Thunder rumbled and lightning forked the sky, continuing for an hour.

By evening the sodden detachment was bone-weary. Dusk was seeping in as they reached a fast-running river and halted on its bank. Most of the men scattered into the adjacent cottonwoods to relieve themselves. Daniel, accompanied by his guard Pedro, did likewise. They found a small clearing, separated from the others by a screen of mesquite. Pedro was scarcely older than Daniel. He lacked the dedication of the previous guard, Alfredo. He sat down on the ground and within a minute was asleep. Daniel's heart began to race. Was this the chance he'd prayed for?

He didn't delay. Making sure he was out of sight of other men, he scrambled to the river-bank and immediately waded into the water. The current, strengthened by the recent rain, was soon drawing him downstream. He ducked beneath the surface for as long as his lungs would permit, coming up to snatch a breath before diving again. How long would it be before his guard awoke? He swam on with all the strength he could muster; it was made harder by the fact that he still wore his boots. He was glad that darkness had fallen rapidly. Presently, he quit the river, feeling the chill of the breeze, and, hearing no sound of pursuit, rested within a tiny cave beneath an overhang of rock.

His body ached with fatigue. He closed his eyes but did not sleep. Time passed.

He knew that so far he had been downright lucky. He wondered if Pedro had been reluctant to admit that he had lost his charge and maybe had carried out his own unsuccessful search, giving Daniel valuable time. However, sooner or later Sergeant Waaz would find out what had happened — and then there'd be hell to pay.

His fears were suddenly confirmed. Awareness gripped him and he whispered, 'Oh, God!'

He strained to listen. Beyond the cave's entrance, he could see the night sky silvered by moonlight. From close by came the clink of iron-shod hoofs and the blowing of horses . . . and Daniel died a small death. The ammonia-pungent whiff of horse urine tainted the air. And then he heard the maniacal voice of Sergeant Waaz blaspheming and cursing his men.

Daniel hugged against the rock, holding his breath, unable to stem his trembling. He wished the rock could absorb him

What would he do if they discovered his hiding place? The cave was a perfect trap. He fought back his fear. He bunched his fists, telling himself that he would die fighting, rather than submit to Waaz's wrath and the terrible torture that Faury had promised.

But within a minute, the sounds grew fainter, melting into the breeze, and he breathed again, guessing that the search party had passed over a ridge above him. How long would it be before they returned? Come daylight, they might find his tracks. He pondered on what he should do, and a vision of Faury's hate-filled face taunted him.

The thought somehow gave him renewed energy. He roused himself and crept from the cave. Then he set off, moving away from the route taken by the riders. He had no horse, no gun, and he had no idea where he was, but he was determined to make the most of his freedom.

Presently, he reached a shadowy mesquite thicket and plunged through it, not heeding the thorns that clawed at him.

19

Elmer raised the blinds on the window, allowing moonlight to illuminate the room. The air that came in through the bullet-shattered glass was tainted with the sour stench of disease. He kept a careful watch on Prado. The Mexican remained on the floor, groaning. In the struggle, both pistols had fallen. Elmer retrieved them. He checked Prado's, found the chamber empty and tossed it aside. He levelled his own gun at the Mexican and said, 'You say you've killed Mateo. Where's his body?'

Prado struggled into a sitting position, cursing his pain. 'Sí, señor. His body . . . it is on the hill, outside of town.' In truth, he wasn't certain of this; he wasn't even sure Mateo was dead, though he hoped he was. He was intent on lulling the American into trusting him. He adopted a submissive manner.

'Take me to his body,' Elmer said.

Prado nodded. 'I may not be able to find it in the dark. We must wait till daylight.'

Elmer resigned himself to remaining there until dawn. He had no desire to blunder about with this man in darkness. 'Why were you hiding up here?' he asked.

'I thought you were Mateo.'

'You said Mateo was dead,' Elmer said.

'I thought you were Mateo's ghost.' Prado replied.

Elmer grunted his disbelief. He asked, 'How come you know Mateo?'

'He killed my brother,' Prado said.

He looked at Elmer, the whites of his pleading eyes showing in the gloom. '*Señor*, I hurt badly. I was mauled by a bear . . . and now, the fight. Can I rest on the bed?'

Elmer said, 'Yes, but no tricks. I'm watching you.'

Prado rose from the floor and settled himself on the bed. Soon he was snoring.

Elmer was puzzled. This man was dressed as a *vaquero*, but he did not seem like a typical Mexican cowboy.

Elmer also felt weary. He seated himself on a chair, but he maintained his watch, his gun ready.

Time passed. He heard the church clock tolling the hours away. He was anxious to quit Amerido, for the place reeked of death. At last the first glimmer of dawn's light showed through the window. He heard the rattling progress of a wagon in the street outside. He rose, went across to the bed and touched the muzzle of his pistol to the Mexican's cheek.

Prado came awake and gazed around with alarmed eyes. Elmer found something familiar about the man, but couldn't determine what it was.

'Let's make a move,' he said. 'It's light enough now.'

Prado nodded and climbed stiffly

from the bed. 'There's no need for the gun, señor. I will not run away.'

Elmer nodded but kept the gun pointed at the Mexican. They left the room and went down the staircase.

'Have you got a horse?' Elmer asked.

'*Sí, señor.* Tethered in the trees at the top of the hill.'

They walked up the deserted street to where Elmer had left his own horse, tied by a water trough. Still keeping Prado covered, he mounted up. 'Lead the way,' he said. 'Take me to Mateo's body.'

The Mexican nodded. They left the ghost of the town, passed the sign warning them to keep out, and presently started to climb the hill. It was growing lighter. Prado was panting from exertion, but inwardly his mind was racing.

When they approached the wreck of the surrey, two turkey vultures rose into the sky. They'd been feeding on the dead horse that still lay between the shafts, its carcass ripped open, exposing ribs and guts.

'Show me Mateo's body.' Elmer demanded.

'Sí. It must be here somewhere.' Prado strode around in the long grass, searching. Suddenly he shouted with excitement, seeing a crumpled heap a few yards off. But as Elmer rode up, Prado groaned with dismay. Here was no body. It was just discarded ecclesiastical clothes.

Gradually it dawned on Prado. Mateo was not here. He had eluded him yet again. Prado grew desperate. He noticed that Elmer had holstered his pistol. An idea came to him. He approached a hollow in the ground, a narrow hole and called out, 'Here!'

The way was too rugged for the horse so Elmer dismounted and joined him.

'Can you see it?' Prado said, pointing down. Elmer stepped forward, momentarily turning his back.

Prado sprang to life, made a grab for the holstered gun. Elmer felt the pistol catch leather as it was lifted. He felt the pressure of the barrel on his arm on the way up. He twisted around, ramming his elbow into the Mexican's belly, doubling him up in agony. The gun went off, the bullet whining harmlessly into thin air. He gripped Prado's pistol-holding hand. He squeezed, cracking the knuckles. Prado dropped the gun, stumbled and then went down. Elmer stooped to retrieve the weapon.

By the time Prado had regained his wind, Elmer had his gun pointed at him. 'You're too slow,' he growled.

The Mexican was sprawled helpless on the ground, his liquid dark eyes hysterical with fear. Elmer aimed his pistol at his head, his finger curled around the trigger. He could have killed him then and would have done so had he realized that he had been part of the gang that had murdered his wife. But his previous association with him had been mostly in the dark and recognition did not come to him.

With the man squarely in his sights, he paused, hearing the whimpered pleas for mercy. *'Por amor de Dios! No, señor!'* Elmer recalled the killings he'd been responsible for when he was in the Rangers and it gave him no pleasure. He had never killed in cold blood. He waited for half a minute, then he turned his gun to the side. 'Get away,' he said. 'I never wanna see you again!'

Prado scrambled to his feet, took one glance at Elmer, then ran off, stumbling, twice falling in his desperate haste. Soon he had disappeared into the trees further up the hill.

★ ★ ★

Daniel had been running for what seemed a lifetime. For a long while he kept mostly to the forest, welcoming its gloom, seeking cover wherever he could. He had swum across rivers; he had no idea where he was going. All he knew was that he had to put as much distance as he could between himself and any pursuers. He tried to convince himself that Sergeant Baca would not have spent too much time hunting for him. He would have had to lead his patrol back to camp. Faury would explode with fury when he learned of the boy's escape. Maybe he would send out a further search party. Daniel felt sorry for Pedro the young *rurale* who had gone to sleep when guarding him. He hoped he wouldn't be punished too severely.

He had quit the trees at mid-morning on the day following that of his escape. He constantly peered into the distance, fearing that he might see a column of *rurales*. Twice he swore he glimpsed riders bobbing up and down but when he blinked hard, he realized they were merely clumps of saguaro that he saw, shimmering in the heat. He prayed that he would soon come to a village where he might find a welcome, but he encountered nothing apart from sprawling desert and cactus, and far off, the hazy streak of hills which could have been a thousand miles away.

Towards noon, with the sun beating down on him, he was exhausted. There was no shade anywhere and he noted that overhead, a turkey vulture had been following him. At last he collapsed close to a towering cactus, curled into a foetus-like position and lapsed into a stupor. The vulture descended, landing a few yards from him, waiting.

A prod in the ribs roused him. He got his eyes open and looked up, but all he could make out, silhouetted against the bright sky, was a looming shadow. He thought: *Baca*! He glanced further afield and as his vision cleared he saw six mounted horsemen, sitting their animals, watching him. He cried out with despair, but then he realized that these men were not wearing *rurale* uniforms. His gaze swung back to the man standing over him. He was not Baca. Daniel saw the beard and the hard, weather-soiled features and the way his powerful shoulders bulged the seams of his sweat-dark calico shirt. He also saw the sheriff's badge pinned to his vest. His horror relented.

'What have we here?' the lawman

demanded in a Texan voice.

Daniel struggled into a sitting position. '*Señor*,' he gasped, 'I am so hungry. Can I please have some food . . . and drink?'

The stranger emitted a deep laugh. 'Get up, boy.'

A minute later Daniel was wolfing down hard crackers and rashers of dried bacon, followed by water from a canteen. Afterwards he related his story to bemused listeners and presently he learned that his benefactors were Bannack County Sheriff Brad Wilshaw and his posse who had come south, having been granted authority from the Mexican government, in pursuit of Luiz Prado, murderer of Sheriff Harlock. Wilshaw was an old acquaintance of Elmer Carrington, and if this boy had been his sidekick, then he reckoned he warranted help.

The sheriff mounted his horse, pulled Daniel up behind him and the posse moved on, heading southward towards Amerido.

20

When Mateo had fallen from the surrey, the horse having been shot, he had hurt his back and had remained hidden in the grass for half an hour, cursing his luck that his disguise of wearing churchman's clothes had not fooled Prado. He was amazed that the man had survived the bear's attack. He guessed it was Prado who had shot at him days earlier.

At first he expected Prado would come looking for him but this did not materialize and he decided to make a move.

The night was flowing in about him. Firstly he returned to the stricken surrey and retrieved his normal clothing into which he changed. Then he found his gunbelt and rifle that he had stowed beneath the seat, and, most importantly, the case in which he had crammed as much of the money as he could carry. The rest he had hidden beneath the floorboards of his house. He started up the hill towards the shadowy trees. He resigned himself to the prospect of the long walk to Vallejo where he had acquaintances who would help him in return for payment.

That was when a sound, coming from the forest, attracted his attention.

Hours ago Prado had left his horse close-hobbled in a clearing. Now, the prowling of some predator alarmed the animal and its nervous whinny carried clearly in the night air. Mateo grunted with satisfaction and changed direction, drawn by the sound. It took him some time to locate the horse, but when he eventually did he also found evidence of the campsite, together with the tack, that had been left.

He was about to gather up the saddle, when an idea came to him. His assailant was sure to return for his horse. Mateo would be ready for him. He extracted the lariat and knife from the tack, and uncoiled the rope. He tossed it up over the branch and adjusted the honda to create a hanging noose. Next, he cut out the narrowest of footholds in the trunk of the tree. He smiled to himself. The man would pay dearly for the inconvenience he had caused. He would walk into a trap from which there would be no escape, not from death, nor from the torture that would precede it.

Mateo waited impatiently through the dark hours. He adopted a position just outside the campsite's perimeter, his Springfield loaded and ready. He did not sleep but listened for sounds and heard the hooting of owls, the calls of coyotes and the occasional stirrings of the horse. Then, as the sun sent slivers of dawn's light through the tangled branches, he heard the blast of a single shot, fired by a handgun. It came from down the hill. He did not move but remained hidden in the undergrowth. Shortly, the panting breath of a running man became audible. When he burst in to the campsite clearing, he presented an almost point-blank target. In that instant Mateo recognized Luiz Prado.

He fired, the bullet slamming into Prado's shoulder, hurling him backwards. He lay upon the ground, screaming with pain. Mateo rose, walked to the writhing body. He pressed the muzzle of his gun against Prado's knee and pulled the trigger, shattering the leg and creating a spasm of agony in the fallen man.

Prado was raving as Mateo dragged him to the tree and slipped the lariat's noose over his head. He placed a further loop around his chest, beneath his armpits. He hauled Prado into an upright position and then hoisted him some two feet off the ground. He pushed his good foot onto the notch he had cut, forcing Prado to support his weight on this. As his blood seeped away, his strength would give out and he would drop, and experience a slow, choking death.

Well satisfied with his work, Mateo saddled the palomino and, gripping his case of money, rode off. He was slippery with Prado's gore but he did not care. His pleasure at stringing Prado up had been somewhat marred by the fact that he himself was not feeling well.

* * *

Twenty-four hours later, Sheriff Bradshaw, his six-man posse and Daniel stood in the clearing, gazing up with a mixture of satisfaction and distaste at the corpse dangling before them. On approaching Amerido, they had been drawn by the circling of buzzards above this spot and they had discovered Luiz Prado, or what was left of him after scavengers had been at work. His body was sodden with blood, but was now covered with a sheen of flies. His foot had slipped from its notch and the rope had strangled him. There was no way of telling the exact moment of death.

'You're certain that's Prado, Brad?' posseman Bud Wilson inquired.

Wilshaw nodded. 'It's him all right. I guess our hunt is over. We can go home.'

There were grunts of delight from his companions.

'We needn't have bothered comin' ,' another man commented. 'Somebody else did the job for us. But who?'

'It don't matter,' the sheriff said. 'It's not our concern. I guess he had plenty of enemies. At least we can confirm he's dead.'

'How will you prove it's him?'

Wilshaw smoothed his beard thoughtfully, then said, 'I'm gonna cut his head off, take it back. That'll prove we're not lying. I guess it'll still be recognizable.'

Everybody, except Daniel, agreed it was a good idea, although nobody volunteered to carry out the decapitation. However Bud Wilson was kind enough to hand the sheriff his big knife.

Later, there was some talk about going to the next town of Vallejo to replenish supplies, Amerido being a no-go destination, but Wilshaw decided against it, saying they would start back for home straight away.

Daniel was not happy with the situation. He had hoped that he could remain under the protection of the posse. He had also hoped that they would help him find Mateo — and even more importantly discover what had happened to Elmer. Now, with the prospect of the lawmen pulling out, he would have to make a decision. Either he could return across the border with the knowledge that his mission had been a failure, or he could stay in Mexico alone, pray that he could steer clear of the *rurales*, try to find his good friend and fulfil his original intention of bringing justice to the man he hated.

For a boy of sixteen the latter prospect would seem daunting. But Daniel no longer considered himself a boy, figuring that his experiences had matured him into a fully-fledged man.

Wilshaw tried to persuade him to

return with them, saying it was crazy for him to stay in Mexico. However, Daniel could be stubborn, and the more they tried to talk him into going back, the more he insisted on staying. His intention would be to go to Vallejo where he felt he would be reasonably safe. Maybe he could earn some money while he formed a plan to complete what Elmer and he had set out to achieve.

Finally, Wilshaw reluctantly agreed to leave him. He and the other members of the posse had grown to like him, for he was a winsome companion. As a farewell token, they gave him a lariat and tack, and perhaps more portentously, a grullo horse that had been used as a pack animal but was equally reliable for riding. Daniel was profoundly grateful and bade them farewell with genuine sadness.

21

After he had let Prado go, Elmer had remained close to Amerido for three days, watching the incoming trail in the hope that Mateo might show up, but he did not.

In the afternoon, he shot a turkey and, using the Indian method, he made a fire with sticks, cooked the bird and assuaged his hunger.

On the third night, he made camp in an oak thicket. He was tired and, with the onset of darkness, he bedded down. But in the small hours, he turned restlessly in his blanket, tortured by a dream that he was back in Amerido and victim of the plague. His body was covered in red spots. Soon he would die, his corpse left in the street for the death cart to collect, after which he would be consigned to a mass grave, forgotten and unmourned.

When a pain awoke him, it took a minute for him to orientate himself. Thank God the dream was nothing more than his brain torturing him. The morning was cool yet he was covered in sweat. Now, through overhead branches, he could see the glimmer of another dawn. *One more day's passed*, he thought, *and Daniel is getting closer to being shot.* And still he had come nowhere near to tracking down Mateo, let alone decapitating him. He shuddered. He ached all over. The fight he'd had with Prado had somehow left him drained. He figured maybe, at fifty-one, he was getting too old for such adventure.

Then he remembered his beloved Lauren, the torment she had suffered, and he knew he would never rest until either he or Mateo was in a grave.

He rose, stiff and cold, and pulled his poncho around his shoulders. He saddled the big sorrel horse and unbuckled the hobbles. It seemed an almighty effort. His legs felt numb and suddenly his breathing became laboured. He leaned against the horse. He tried to shrug off his grogginess, tried to convince himself that it was nothing serious. He knew he would need all his concentration if he was to keep watch on the trail into Amerido. His hope was still that Mateo would attempt to return to the town, go back to his house and the hoard of cash that was surely hidden within it. Mateo had to be stopped, preferably by a bullet in the head. No, Elmer told himself, not the head. That had to be preserved for Faury.

Nausea came upon him and he vomited up the food he had in his belly. Afterwards, he pulled the leg of his Levi's out of his boot and gazed at the inside of his knee. It was there that he saw the two red spots.

Now, his vision was blurred. He slumped to the ground, fell back and slipped into unconsciousness.

For a while the big sorrel waited, as if puzzled by events, but then a sparrow hawk flapped skywards from a nearby branch and this spooked the animal and he trotted off, gradually gaining speed. He was soon gone.

★ ★ ★

Daniel spotted the horse a half hour later, grazing on the sparse grass. He noticed that he was still saddled and this intrigued him. Every time he approached the big animal, he edged away but did not gallop off. He showed an interest in the *grullo*. Eventually Daniel got close enough to grab the trailing reins and was then able to pacify him with soothing words and a gentle pat of the withers.

He saw the weapon sheathed in the saddle scabbard. When he drew it out, his heart began to beat faster. He'd only seen one .44 Henry Repeater before and that had belonged to Elmer! His mind was suddenly racing. Did this mean that Elmer had fallen from his mount? Did this mean he was close by?

Daniel bridled his excitement as another possibility occurred to him. Maybe the gun had been stolen. Maybe Elmer was dead.

He led both animals to a nearby tree and tethered them. He circled around for ten minutes before he found what he sought — the tracks of the big sorrel. They showed clearly in the earth. If he followed them back . . . what would he learn?

He retrieved the two horses and picked up the trail. He lost it twice over patches of rock, but to his relief he found it again.

When he finally discovered Elmer sprawled on the ground, he didn't know whether to shout for joy or cry with despair. For a dreadful moment, he thought Elmer was lifeless, but then he saw the faint movement of his chest. He gripped his shoulder and to his relief Elmer's eyes opened and registered recognition.

'What's happened?' Daniel gasped.

Elmer attempted to respond but his

words wouldn't come. His lips and tongue seemed swollen. He raised his arm, tried to wave Daniel away.

The plague, he thought, *he's caught the plague!*

He felt like dying himself, dying alongside Elmer. He felt utterly desperate. What could he do? But then he goaded himself into thinking. Sheriff Wilshaw and his men had discussed going to a place called Vallejo, which wasn't far off. If he could somehow get Elmer there, they might find a doctor.

Elmer was in no condition to ride a horse but an idea came to Daniel. For an hour he laboured, breaking off branches and tying them together with his rope. He checked Elmer frequently, but he only gazed at him with wide eyes and gestured for him to stay away.

Finally Daniel was satisfied with his work. He had fashioned a crude travois and he attached this to the big sorrel and spread his poncho across it. He returned to Elmer, dragged him up onto his unsteady legs and, ignoring his reluctance, persuaded him to take the few stumbling steps to the travois. Further effort had him lying back, tied to it.

Daniel mounted the *grullo* and, leading the sorrel, started off. Being dragged along, it was a rough ride for Elmer but he was in no condition to complain.

Presently, they passed a fingerpost indicating they were going the right way for Vallejo.

By the time they had passed through outlying fields where goats and sheep grazed, and Daniel saw the white buildings of the town ahead, the travois was disintegrating and he was afraid Elmer would fall off. Shortly they reached a half-ruined adobe. It was deserted, well out of town and standing alone. It had obviously been abandoned long ago. Beside it was a wrecked ox cart, its wooden wheels broken. Daniel decided to leave Elmer in the adobe, go into town and attempt to find a doctor. He explained this to Elmer, who now seemed much brighter and nodded his understanding.

★ ★ ★

Doctor Felipe Cabello served the community of Vallejo and was much respected by rich and poor alike. He was a tall, thin man with a studious manner who had qualified forty years ago at the Academy of Medicine, but he had learned more by treating *rancheros* and peons in poor communities. He was also a self-taught veterinarian and specialized in reviving birds injured in the popular local activity of cock-fighting.

When Señor Eduardo Anza called to see him, he was horrified by the state of the man, who complained of vomiting and repeated diarrhoea. His appearance was ghastly; his colour was grey, his eyes sunken deep in their sockets. His heartbeat was rapid, as was his pulse. When Doctor Cabello saw the red spots, his worst fears were confirmed.

Anza had the plague and must leave Vallejo immediately before contamination spread.

Anza accepted his orders to quit the town with a curt nod. His manner seemed to imply that he blamed the doctor for his sorry state of affairs. But Cabello showed professional patience. Perhaps he would have been less sympathetic had he realized that Anza was also known as Mateo.

'You must rest,' the doctor advised. 'Go to the derelict adobe outside of town. The one with the wrecked ox cart outside. Stay there and I will come and treat you this evening. You must avoid all contact with other people.'

Anza paid and staggered out, showing no gratitude. Cabello had felt a distinct dislike for him.

Elmer sat inside the adobe, his back against the wall, and waited for Daniel's return. A change had come over him. The swelling of his lips and tongue had gone down, the strength in his legs had returned, his vision had cleared and within him was the confidence that he would not die. He rose to his feet, and only after he had paced around within the walls three times did he feel the necessity to rest down again.

It was then that a figure appeared in the open doorway. Mateo had heard movement inside the adobe, and, forever expecting trouble, came in gun first. The two men gazed at each other, both stunned as recognition dawned.

Elmer expressed his feelings first. The word burst from him as if of its own accord. '*Bastard*!'

Mateo swayed on his feet and despite his sickness a look of triumph spread across his face.

'Elmer Carrington,' he snarled. 'I have waited a long time for this. You escaped me once. You'll never do it again.'

'You raped and strangled my wife,' Elmer said. 'You'll rot in hell for that.'

Somehow, Mateo mustered a contemptuous laugh.

Elmer felt dismay. He had loaned

Daniel his pistol in case he needed it in town. His Henry Repeater was leaning against the wall alongside him. He had no doubt that if he tried to grab it, Mateo would shoot him.

'I wish I could torture you, *amigo*,' Mateo leered. 'I wish I could slit you open, tie your guts to a horse's tail and watch you unravel — ha! But there's no time . . . no time. Say goodbye to this world.'

His look was insane as he raised his pistol and Elmer found himself gazing into the muzzle's unblinking borehole.

22

Daniel fired in haste, the big Colt kicking back in his hand. The squat, bandy figure of the man and the voice had been unmistakable. Mateo screamed as the bullet slammed into his back and he was catapulted forward, landing face down. Elmer grabbed his rifle and scrambled up. Blood was oozing from Mateo's wound and he was emitting a loud, groaning sound.

Elmer kept his gun pointed at him, never trusting him. He nodded his profound thanks to Daniel. 'You've saved my life twice today. I'll never forget that. Thank God you came.'

Daniel smiled, a proud glint in his eye. 'It was an honour, Captain.'

'Can you get me the rope?' Elmer asked.

The boy nodded, went outside, unhooked the lariat from the grullo's saddle-horn and returned. Elmer took the lariat, uncoiled it and then slipped the loop around the unresisting Mateo, passing it beneath his armpits. He pulled it tight. Daniel sensed what was coming and together they dragged the still-breathing Mateo outside to where the horses were grazing. Leaving some slack, Elmer fastened the end of the rope to the saddle-horn of the big sorrel. He was still unsteady, still faintly dizzy, but he got his foot in the stirrup and hauled himself onto the horse's back. Then he dug his heels in and they started off at a fast clip, soon becoming a gallop.

Mateo screamed once as the rope was drawn taught. He was dragged over the rugged ground, bumping up and down like a rag doll, leaving a trail of blood in his wake.

Elmer circled the adobe six times, when, panting, he finally reined in and fell from the horse. Daniel rushed to where Mateo lay, his pistol ready, but it was not needed. This evil man would never again terrorize innocent folk.

Elmer had risen to his feet, still unstable. He took no pride in killing Mateo, but the face of Lauren had been in his mind, and with it the terrible wrench of losing her and everything they had worked for. Revenge was not sweet, but it was something he'd sworn to do. Now perhaps her soul could rest in peace.

There was still the thought that the disease might be spread, so it was decided that Daniel would return to the town for food. Meanwhile Elmer sat in the adobe, the rifle slanted across his knees. The prospect of trouble still haunted him, but none came. A half hour later, Daniel was back, accompanied by Doctor Cabello.

Daniel had explained the entire situation to the medical man, who had at first been reluctant to believe that the person he had diagnosed with the plague and had since been killed, was a notorious bandit, but gradually he became convinced. He arrived at the derelict adobe fully prepared to treat another victim of the disease.

Elmer started to rise, but Cabello, speaking good English, told him to stay where he was.

'Please take off your shirt,' he instructed, and when Elmer complied, he listened to his chest with a stethoscope, then asked a number of quick-fire questions, nodding as the expected answers came. Next, he had him remove his boot and roll up his Levi's, exposing a single red spot.

'That's strange,' Elmer said. 'There were two spots last time I looked.'

The doctor smiled. 'A typical symptom. Your vision was blurred. You were seeing double.'

'Is it the plague?' Elmer inquired anxiously.

'No. You were the victim of *centruroides sculpturatus*.'

'What the hell is that, Doc?'

You were bitten by a bark scorpion, and a mighty vicious one by the look of things. I have never known such intense symptoms. It is not contagious. I will give you some opiates. You should feel completely better in a couple of days.'

As the truth sank in, Elmer sighed with relief. Standing watching, Daniel was overcome, tears of joy streaming down his cheeks.

'The best thing you can do,' Cabello said, 'is go into town and have a good meal. I'll make sure you are made welcome.'

Elmer shook the doctor's hand, finding words inadequate to express his gratitude.

He and Daniel stayed in Vallejo for three days, enjoying rest and good food. True to the prognosis, Elmer recovered completely and, on his knees, he thanked the Lord for their salvation and prayed for those folk who had suffered in the plague. Cabello ensured his guests were treated with the utmost hospitality. They left with great sadness. The journey back was long. Mercifully, they encountered no *rurales*, nor any hazards that they could not overcome.

They were jubilant, their mission completed. Daniel was to attain his ambition to become a Texas Ranger; Elmer would put flowers on Lauren's grave, maybe explain to her all that had happened, then he would open his soul to whatever the future might bring.

THE END

We do hope that you have enjoyed reading this large print book.

Did you know that all of our titles are available for purchase?

We publish a wide range of high quality large print books including:
Romances, Mysteries, Classics
General Fiction
Non Fiction and Westerns

Special interest titles available in large print are:
The Little Oxford Dictionary
Music Book, Song Book
Hymn Book, Service Book

Also available from us courtesy of Oxford University Press:
Young Readers' Dictionary
(large print edition)
Young Readers' Thesaurus
(large print edition)

For further information or a free brochure, please contact us at:
Ulverscroft Large Print Books Ltd.,
The Green, Bradgate Road, Anstey,
Leicester, LE7 7FU, England.
Tel: (00 44) **0116 236 4325**
Fax: (00 44) **0116 234 0205**

DOUBLE CROSS TRAIL DRIVE

Chet Cunningham

The journey begins as an ordinary trail drive from Texas to the railroad in Kansas — but soon turns deadly as bullets fly and rustlers try to steal the whole herd of steer . . . Back at the ranch in Texas, the violence continues, as the ranch owner seems to have become a sitting target. Whoever is out to ruin the ranch and kill the owner must be discovered, especially as the final deadly cattle stampede threatens to settle the matter once and for all . . .

DUEL OF SHADOWS

Billy Hall

Eli Lowenstein has been murdered, and Sam Murray wasn't the man who took his life. But when the accusers threaten to look in his saddle-bags, he remembers the strange noises he heard that night, and the talk of the planted evidence that had condemned Ephraim Harris to an untimely lynching. He's sure that if they find anything he'll swing from the end of a rope, just like old Ephraim. And there's no way Sam Murray is going to sit back and let them slip that noose over his head . . .

TROOPER DALTON

Ed Law

When Dalton is offered the opportunity to sign up with the Plains Cavalry, as an alternative to a prison sentence, he joins Company H — known as Company Hell — but soon regrets his decision. The troopers are a motley collection of prisoners recruited from jailhouses and gunslingers running from arrest warrants. As his fellow troopers are more determined to destroy the peace than to keep it, Dalton will need all his survival skills to serve out his term, and all his ingenuity to defeat their plans.